A ZOMBIE
CHRISTMAS
CAROL

First published in the United Kingdom in 2011
by Swordworks Books

ISBN 978-1906512668

Typeset by Swordworks Books
Printed and bound in the UK & US
A catalogue record of this book is available
from the British Library

Cover design by Swordworks Books
www.swordworks.co.uk

A ZOMBIE CHRISTMAS CAROL

MICHAEL G. THOMAS
CHARLES DICKENS

STAVE ONE

MARLEY'S GHOST.

Marley was dead: to begin with. There is no doubt whatever about that. Since that dreadful episode at the National Provincial Bank seven years ago there were few who had not heard of the greed and the downfall of Marley. The very manner of his death spun into a bewildering array of legends but all contained the same basic truth. His death was a result of the character defect of that toad of a man and he had died like so many on that infamous night, the night the dead rose and walked the streets of London.

The register of his burial was signed by the clergyman, the clerk, the coroner, the undertaker, and the chief mourner. Any death that occurred in such a violent and public manner was simply a matter of public record. Scrooge signed it: and Scrooge's name was good upon

'Change, for anything he chose to put his hand to. Old Marley was as dead as a door-nail.

Mind! I don't mean to say that I know, of my own knowledge, what there is particularly dead about a door-nail. I might have been inclined, myself, to regard a coffin-nail as the deadest piece of ironmongery in the trade. From my knowledge of those things most unnatural I feel I have a better understanding of the dead, the living and even the living dead!

But the wisdom of our ancestors is in the simile; and my unhallowed hands shall not disturb it, or the Country's done for. You will therefore permit me to repeat, emphatically, that Marley was as dead as a door-nail and unlike certain other dead things would not be strolling the lanes and streets of the land.

Scrooge knew he was dead? Of course he did. How could it be otherwise? Scrooge and he were partners for I don't know how many years and he had been there at the very end of Marley's days on this earth. Though he would never discuss the subject, Scrooge had seen Marley's death and it was something he wanted to forget more than anything else in his life. Scrooge was his sole executor, his sole administrator, his sole assign, his sole residuary legatee, his sole friend, and following the extraordinary events seven years ago, the sole mourner. And even Scrooge was not so dreadfully cut up by the sad event, but that he was an excellent man of business on the very day of the funeral, and solemnised it with an undoubted bargain.

The mention of Marley's funeral brings me back to the point I started from. There is no doubt that Marley was dead. Yes, it is well known that Marley was killed by those that are neither living or dead, but it is also well recorded that he died in sight of Scrooge and the pitiful few that made it out of the Bank building that day. In fact, the events that occurred that day are still confused. This must be distinctly understood, or nothing wonderful can come of the story I am going to relate. If we were not perfectly convinced that Hamlet's Father died and could never again rise before the play began, there would be nothing more remarkable in his taking a stroll at night, in an easterly wind, upon his own ramparts, than there would be in any other middle-aged gentleman rashly turning out after dark in a breezy spot—say Saint Paul's Churchyard for instance—literally to astonish his son's weak mind.

Even though Scrooge had watched his partner die in a most terrible manner, he never painted out Old Marley's name. There it stood, years afterwards, above the warehouse door: Scrooge and Marley. The firm was known as Scrooge and Marley. Sometimes people new to the business called Scrooge Scrooge, and sometimes Marley, but he answered to both names. It was all the same to him. Even seven years prior, during the attack on the Bank, few could have told the two men apart as their insatiable appetite for riches and disinterest in the affairs of others became almost legendary.

Oh! Scrooge was a man who wanted for little but he was a tight-fisted hand at the grindstone, Scrooge! a squeezing, wrenching, grasping, scraping, clutching, covetous, old sinner! Hard and sharp as flint, from which no steel had ever struck out generous fire; secret, and self-contained, and solitary as an oyster. The cold within him froze his old features, nipped his pointed nose, shrivelled his cheek, stiffened his gait; made his eyes red, his thin lips blue; and spoke out shrewdly in his grating voice. A frosty rime was on his head, and on his eyebrows, and his wiry chin. He carried his own low temperature always about with him; he iced his office in the dog-days; and didn't thaw it one degree at Christmas.

External heat and cold had little influence on Scrooge. No warmth could warm, no wintry weather chill him. No wind that blew was bitterer than he, no falling snow was more intent upon its purpose, no pelting rain less open to entreaty. Foul weather didn't know where to have him. The heaviest rain, and snow, and hail, and sleet, could boast of the advantage over him in only one respect. They often "came down" handsomely, and Scrooge never did.

Nobody ever stopped him in the street to say, with gladsome looks, "My dear Scrooge, how are you? When will you come to see me?" No beggars implored him to bestow a trifle, no children asked him what it was o'clock, no man or woman ever once in all his life inquired the way to such and such a place, of Scrooge. Even the blind men's dogs appeared to know him; and when they saw him coming on, would tug their owners into doorways and up courts; and then would wag their tails as though they said, "No eye at all is better than an evil eye, dark master!"

But what did Scrooge care! It was the very thing he liked. To edge his way along the crowded paths of life, warning all human sympathy to keep its distance, was what the knowing ones call "nuts" to Scrooge. Whether he faced the living or the dead, old man or child, Scrooge simply wanted to be left alone so that he could get on with the important endeavour of accumulating more money.

Once upon a time—of all the good days in the year, on Christmas Eve—old Scrooge sat busy in his counting-house. It was cold, bleak, biting weather: foggy withal: and he could hear the people in the court outside, go wheezing up and down, beating their hands upon their breasts, and stamping their feet upon the pavement stones to warm them. The city clocks had only just gone three, but it was quite dark already—it had not been light all day—and candles were flaring in the windows of the neighbouring offices, like ruddy smears upon the palpable brown air. The fog came pouring in at every chink and keyhole, and was so dense without, that although the court was of the narrowest, the houses opposite were mere phantoms. To see the dingy cloud come drooping down, obscuring everything, one might have thought that Nature lived hard by, and was brewing on a large scale.

It was about this time that the most significant attack by the damned was to occur, but for now, only those on their way to the dockland would feel the brunt of the assault. Events would conspire however to spread their evil across many parts of the city and Scrooge himself would feel the fear that only the undead could inspire. If only the inhabitants of London had known what was coming that Christmas they may very well have abandoned the city to its fate.

The door of Scrooge's counting-house was open that he might keep his eye upon his clerk, who in a dismal little cell beyond, a sort of tank, was copying letters. Scrooge had a very small fire, but the clerk's fire was so very much smaller that it looked like one coal. But he couldn't replenish it, for Scrooge kept the coal-box in his own room; and so surely as the clerk came in with the shovel, the master predicted that it would be necessary for them to part. Wherefore the clerk put on his white comforter, and tried to warm himself at the candle; in which effort, not being a man of a strong imagination, he failed.

The single sacrifice to the emptiness of the room was a small selection of artefacts hanging on the wall. One of the most interesting was the old military cavalry sword that rumour had it said Scrooge had used when he and Marley had served with the yeomanry. This was a long time ago however and the London and Westminster Light Horse were one of the many subjects that Scrooge would never talk about, so that many people that knew of him assumed it was nothing but a tall tale. How much truth there was to some of the stories will hardly be known as the unit itself was in a constant state of being formed and disbanded.

"A merry Christmas, uncle! God save you!" cried a cheerful voice. It was the voice of Scrooge's nephew, who came upon him so quickly that this was the first intimation he had of his approach. The young man looked up in awe at the selection of weapons on the wall though, like everybody else, he had no idea if they had ever seen any kind of use but in his heart, he hoped it had been something exciting. He had broached the subject many times before but no person had anything of note to pass on other than the two old misers might have used them in the past. They were hardly the most exciting of conversations.

"Bah!" said Scrooge, "Humbug!"

He had so heated himself with rapid walking in the fog and frost, this nephew of Scrooge's, that he was all in a glow; his face was ruddy and handsome; his eyes sparkled, and his breath smoked again.

"Christmas a humbug, uncle!" said Scrooge's nephew. "You don't mean that, I am sure?"

"I do," said Scrooge. "Merry Christmas! What right have you to be merry? What reason have you to be merry?

You're poor enough."

"Come, then," returned the nephew gaily. "What right have you to be dismal? What reason have you to be morose? You're rich enough."

Scrooge having no better answer ready on the spur of the moment, said, "Bah!" again; and followed it up with "Humbug."

"Don't be cross, uncle!" said the nephew.

"What else can I be," returned the uncle, "when I live in such a world of fools as this? Merry Christmas! Out upon merry Christmas! What's Christmas time to you but a time for paying bills without money; a time for finding yourself a year older, but not an hour richer; a time for balancing your books and having every item in 'em through a round dozen of months presented dead against you? If I could work my will," said Scrooge indignantly, "every idiot who goes about with 'Merry Christmas' on his lips, should be boiled with his own pudding, and buried with a stake of holly through his heart. He should!"

"Uncle!" pleaded the nephew.

"Nephew!" returned the uncle sternly, "keep Christmas in your own way, and let me keep it in mine."

"Keep it!" repeated Scrooge's nephew. "But you don't keep it."

"Let me leave it alone, then," said Scrooge. "Much good may it do you! Much good it has ever done you!"

"There are many things from which I might have

derived good, by which I have not profited, I dare say," returned the nephew. "Christmas among the rest. But I am sure I have always thought of Christmas time, when it has come round—apart from the veneration due to its sacred name and origin, if anything belonging to it can be apart from that—as a good time; a kind, forgiving, charitable, pleasant time; the only time I know of, in the long calendar of the year, when men and women seem by one consent to open their shut-up hearts freely, and to think of people below them as if they really were fellow-passengers to the grave, and not another race of creatures bound on other journeys. And therefore, uncle, though it has never put a scrap of gold or silver in my pocket, I believe that it has done me good, and will do me good; and I say, God bless it!"

The clerk in the Tank involuntarily applauded. Becoming immediately sensible of the impropriety, he poked the fire, and extinguished the last frail spark for ever.

"Let me hear another sound from you," said Scrooge, "and you'll keep your Christmas by losing your situation! You're quite a powerful speaker, sir," he added, turning to his nephew. "I wonder you don't go into Parliament."

"Don't be angry, uncle. Come! Dine with us to-morrow."

Scrooge said that he would see him—yes, indeed he did. He went the whole length of the expression, and said that he would see him in that extremity first.

"But why?" cried Scrooge's nephew. "Why?"

"Why did you get married?" said Scrooge.

"Because I fell in love."

"Because you fell in love!" growled Scrooge, as if that were the only one thing in the world more ridiculous than a merry Christmas. "Good afternoon!"

"Nay, uncle, but you never came to see me before that happened. Why give it as a reason for not coming now?"

"Good afternoon," said Scrooge.

"I want nothing from you; I ask nothing of you; why cannot we be friends?"

"Good afternoon," said Scrooge.

"I am sorry, with all my heart, to find you so resolute. We have never had any quarrel, to which I have been a party. But I have made the trial in homage to Christmas, and I'll keep my Christmas humour to the last. So A Merry Christmas, uncle!"

"Good afternoon!" said Scrooge.

"And A Happy New Year!"

"Good afternoon!" said Scrooge.

His nephew left the room without an angry word, notwithstanding. He stopped at the outer door to bestow the greetings of the season on the clerk, who, cold as he was, was warmer than Scrooge; for he returned them cordially.

"There's another fellow," muttered Scrooge; who

overheard him: "my clerk, with fifteen shillings a week, and a wife and family, talking about a merry Christmas. I'll retire to Bedlam."

This lunatic, in letting Scrooge's nephew out, had let two other people in. They were portly gentlemen, pleasant to behold, and now stood, with their hats off, in Scrooge's office. They had books and papers in their hands, and bowed to him.

"Scrooge and Marley's, I believe," said one of the gentlemen, referring to his list. "Have I the pleasure of addressing Mr. Scrooge, or Mr. Marley?"

"Mr. Marley has been dead these seven years," Scrooge replied. "He died seven years ago, this very night."

"Good Lord," said the first gentleman as he turned to his comrade. With a look of surprise, he turned back to Scrooge.

"Am I to understand that you and Mr. Marley were present at the outbreak in the National Provincial Bank seven years ago? I thought only some of the army were left alive after the battle?" he asked somewhat sceptically.

"Damn your pertinence man, yes we were there and yes Mr. Marley died a most miserable death. A death I would rather not waste time dwelling on. What do you want, sir?" said an exasperated Scrooge.

The gentleman, though a little taken aback by Scrooge's outburst, was encouraged by his partner to continue.

"Well then, with regards to Mr. Marley we have no

doubt his liberality is well represented by his surviving partner," said the gentleman, presenting his credentials as he smiled uncomfortably to Scrooge.

It certainly was; for they had been two kindred spirits. At the ominous word "liberality," Scrooge frowned, and shook his head, and handed the credentials back though the two gentlemen, unaccustomed as they were to Scrooge, they continued their discussion, assuming that he might at the very least be intrigued to hear what they had to say.

"At this festive season of the year, Mr. Scrooge," said the gentleman, taking up a pen, "it is more than usually desirable that we should make some slight provision for the Poor and destitute, who suffer greatly at the present time. Many thousands are in want of common necessaries; hundreds of thousands are in want of common comforts, sir. Even though we made it through the awful outbreak that you, sir, were obviously part of, there are many that still suffer, some from the wounds and troubles they inherited from that very struggle."

"Are there no prisons?" asked Scrooge.

"Plenty of prisons," said the gentleman, laying down the pen again.

"Are the dead no longer walking the streets? Is not the city safe from their bloodthirsty menace?" asked Scrooge.

"Indeed, sir. The last of them were destroyed many years ago and none have been seen since," said the second gentleman.

"And the Union workhouses?" demanded Scrooge. "Are they still in operation?"

"They are. Still," returned the gentleman, "I wish I could say they were not."

"The Treadmill and the Poor Law are in full vigour, then?" said Scrooge.

"Both very busy, sir."

"Oh! I was afraid, from what you said at first, that something had occurred to stop them in their useful course," said Scrooge. "I'm very glad to hear it."

"Under the impression that they scarcely furnish Christian cheer of mind or body to the multitude," returned the gentleman, "a few of us are endeavouring to raise a fund to buy the Poor some meat and drink, and means of warmth. We choose this time, because it is a time, of all others, when Want is keenly felt, and Abundance rejoices. What shall I put you down for?"

"Nothing!" Scrooge replied.

"You wish to be anonymous?"

"I wish to be left alone," said Scrooge. "Since you ask me what I wish, gentlemen, that is my answer. I don't make merry myself at Christmas and I can't afford to make idle people merry. I have done my part already by not being killed by those unbreathing monsters. With me alive my money helps to support the establishments I have mentioned—they cost enough; and those who are badly off must go there."

"Many can't go there; and many would rather die."

"If they would rather die," said Scrooge, "they had better do it, and decrease the surplus population. It was surplus population if you remember that provided the fuel to the monstrous outbreak those seven years ago! Besides—excuse me—I don't know that."

"But you might know it," observed the gentleman.

"It's not my business," Scrooge returned. "It's enough for a man to understand his own business, and not to interfere with other people's. Mine occupies me constantly. Good afternoon, gentlemen!"

Seeing clearly that it would be useless to pursue their point, the gentlemen withdrew. Scrooge resumed his labours with an improved opinion of himself, and in a more facetious temper than was usual with him.

Meanwhile the fog and darkness thickened so, that people ran about with flaring links, proffering their services to go before horses in carriages, and conduct them on their way. The ancient tower of a church, whose gruff old bell was always peeping slily down at Scrooge out of a Gothic window in the wall, became invisible, and struck the hours and quarters in the clouds, with tremulous vibrations afterwards as if its teeth were chattering in its frozen head up there.

The cold became intense. In the main street, at the corner of the court, some labourers were repairing the gas-pipes, and had lighted a great fire in a brazier, round which a party of ragged men and boys were gathered: warming their hands and winking their eyes before the blaze in rapture. The water-plug being left in solitude, its overflowings sullenly congealed, and turned to misanthropic ice. The brightness of the shops where holly sprigs and berries crackled in the lamp heat of the windows, made pale faces ruddy as they passed. Poulterers' and grocers' trades became a splendid joke: a glorious pageant, with which it was next to impossible to believe that such dull principles as bargain and sale had anything to do.

The Lord Mayor, in the stronghold of the mighty Mansion House, gave orders to his fifty cooks and butlers to keep Christmas as a Lord Mayor's household should; and even the little tailor, whom he had fined five shillings on the previous Monday for being drunk and bloodthirsty in the streets, stirred up to-morrow's pudding in his garret, while his lean wife and the baby sallied out to buy the beef.

Foggier yet, and colder. Piercing, searching, biting cold. If the good Saint Dunstan had but nipped the Evil Spirit's nose with a touch of such weather as that, instead of using his familiar weapons, then indeed he would have roared to lusty purpose. The owner of one scant young nose, gnawed and mumbled by the hungry cold as bones are gnawed by dogs, stooped down at Scrooge's keyhole to regale him with a Christmas carol: but at the first sound of:

"God bless you, merry gentleman!
May nothing you dismay!"

Scrooge seized the ruler with such energy of action, that the singer fled in terror, leaving the keyhole to the fog and even more congenial frost.

At length the hour of shutting up the counting-house arrived. With an ill-will Scrooge dismounted from his stool, and tacitly admitted the fact to the expectant clerk in the Tank, who instantly snuffed his candle out, and put on his hat.

"You'll want all day to-morrow, I suppose?" said Scrooge.

"If quite convenient, sir."

"It's not convenient," said Scrooge, "and it's not fair. If I was to stop half-a-crown for it, you'd think yourself ill-used, I'll be bound?"

The clerk smiled faintly.

"And yet," said Scrooge, "you don't think me ill-used, when I pay a day's wages for no work."

The clerk observed that it was only once a year.

"A poor excuse for picking a man's pocket every twenty-fifth of December!" said Scrooge, buttoning his great-coat to the chin. "But I suppose you must have the whole day. Be here all the earlier next morning."

The clerk promised that he would; and Scrooge walked out with a growl. The office was closed in a twinkling, and the clerk, with the long ends of his white comforter dangling below his waist (for he boasted no great-coat), went down a slide on Cornhill, at the end of a lane of boys, twenty times, in honour of its being Christmas Eve, and then ran home to Camden Town as hard as he could pelt, to play at blindman's-buff.

If Scrooge had bothered to lift his eyes from his route home, he would have noticed the first signs of evil starting to spread into the dark spaces of the streets. An insidious evil was making its way through the city, seeking the dead or those close to their passing. Each minute that passed seemed to make the evil stronger. In the shadows of a derelict tavern lay a heavily laden cart with several clothed figures slumped across its bed. There was no sign of the animals that would normally pull such as heavy load and underneath the spoked wheels ran a dark trail of blood. It was this cart that had come from the docks that would bring so much calamity to this story. The trail of blood continued off into the distance towards the infamous Bank.

Scrooge however noticed none of this and took his melancholy dinner in his usual melancholy tavern; and having read all the newspapers, and beguiled the rest of the evening with his Banker's-book, went home to bed. He lived in chambers which had once belonged to his deceased partner. They were a gloomy suite of rooms, in a lowering pile of building up a yard, where it had so little business to be, that one could scarcely help fancying it must have run there when it was a young house, playing at hide-and-seek with other houses, and forgotten the way out again. It was old enough now, and dreary enough, for nobody lived in it but Scrooge, the other rooms being all let out as offices. The yard was so dark that even Scrooge, who knew its every stone, was fain to grope with his hands. The fog and frost so hung about the black old gateway of the house, that it seemed as if the Genius of the Weather sat in mournful meditation on the threshold.

Like his counting house, there were few items or artefacts bar those required of necessity. Near the door lay his stick and propped as well near the door were a selection of old military relics that were rusting away. An old musket lay on the floor though it lacked a flint or any ammunition of note. It is doubtful it would have worked anyway with the amount of dust and rust on the moving parts it was probably more a danger to the firer than any hostile target.

Now, it is a fact, that there was nothing at all particular about the knocker on the door, except that it was very large. It is also a fact, that Scrooge had seen it, night and morning, during his whole residence in that place; also that Scrooge had as little of what is called fancy about him as any man in the city of London, even including—

which is a bold word—the corporation, aldermen, and livery. Let it also be borne in mind that Scrooge had not bestowed one thought on Marley, since his last mention of his seven years' dead partner that afternoon. And then let any man explain to me, if he can, how it happened that Scrooge, having his key in the lock of the door, saw in the knocker, without its undergoing any intermediate process of change—not a knocker, but Marley's face, the face that he had last seen alive under a mass of the living dead before being torn apart by tooth and claw.

Marley's face. It was not in impenetrable shadow as the other objects in the yard were, but had a dismal light about it, like a bad lobster in a dark cellar. It was not angry or ferocious, but looked at Scrooge as Marley used to look: with ghostly spectacles turned up on its ghostly forehead. The hair was curiously stirred, as if by breath or hot air; and, though the eyes were wide open, they were perfectly motionless. That, and its livid colour, made it horrible; but its horror seemed to be in spite of the face and beyond its control, rather than a part of its own expression. Down the side of Marley's face were a number of small wounds and a scar ran along his cheek, presumably from wounds he suffered during his attack and death.

As Scrooge looked fixedly at this phenomenon, it was a knocker again.

To say that he was not startled, or that his blood was not conscious of a terrible sensation to which it had been a stranger from infancy, would be untrue. But he put his hand upon the key he had relinquished, turned it sturdily, walked in, and lighted his candle.

He did pause, with a moment's irresolution, before he shut the door; and he did look cautiously behind it first, as if he half expected to be terrified with the sight of Marley's pigtail sticking out into the hall. But there was nothing on the back of the door, except the screws and nuts that held the knocker on, so he said "Pooh, pooh!" and closed it with a bang.

The sound resounded through the house like thunder. Every room above, and every cask in the wine-merchant's cellars below, appeared to have a separate peal of echoes of its own. Scrooge was not a man to be frightened by echoes. He fastened the door, and walked across the hall, and up the stairs; slowly too: trimming his candle as he went.

You may talk vaguely about driving a coach-and-six up a good old flight of stairs, or through a bad young Act of Parliament; but I mean to say you might have got a hearse up that staircase, and taken it broadwise, with the splinter-bar towards the wall and the door towards the balustrades: and done it easy. There was plenty of width for that, and room to spare; which is perhaps the reason why Scrooge thought he saw a locomotive hearse going on before him in the gloom. Half-a-dozen gas-lamps out of the street wouldn't have lighted the entry too well, so you may suppose that it was pretty dark with Scrooge's dip.

Up Scrooge went, not caring a button for that. Darkness is cheap, and Scrooge liked it. But before he shut his heavy door, he removed one of the old cavalry swords from the wall and held it up to his shoulder. It was a simple move but he looked strangely at ease with the old weapon that now lay in both a comfortable position but also ideally placed to use in anger if required. He walked through his rooms to see that all was right. He had just enough recollection of the face to desire to do that whilst keeping his right hand firmly on the weapon, just in case. The weapon gave him a re-assuring, safe feeling though it did nothing to hold back the coldness of the house.

Sitting-room, bedroom, lumber-room. All as they should be. Nobody under the table, nobody under the sofa; a small fire in the grate; spoon and basin ready; and the little saucepan of gruel (Scrooge had a cold in his head) upon the hob. Nobody under the bed; nobody in the closet; nobody in his dressing-gown, which was hanging up in a suspicious attitude against the wall. Lumber-room as usual. Old fire-guard, old shoes, two fish-baskets, washing-stand on three legs, and a poker.

Quite satisfied, he placed the sword down and then closed his door, and locked himself in; double-locked himself in, which was not his custom. Thus secured against surprise, he took off his cravat; put on his dressing-gown and slippers, and his nightcap; and sat down before the fire to take his gruel. To the side of his bed lay a fine bladed dagger though like all of Scrooge's possessions it was old, poorly cared for and saw little if any use.

It was a very low fire indeed; nothing on such a bitter night. He was obliged to sit close to it, and brood over it, before he could extract the least sensation of warmth from such a handful of fuel. The fireplace was an old one, built by some Dutch merchant long ago, and paved all round with quaint Dutch tiles, designed to illustrate the Scriptures. There were Cains and Abels, Pharaoh's daughters; Queens of Sheba, Angelic messengers descending through the air on clouds like feather-beds, Abrahams, Belshazzars, Apostles putting off to sea in butter-boats, hundreds of figures to attract his thoughts; and yet that face of Marley, seven years dead, came like the ancient Prophet's rod, and swallowed up the whole. If each smooth tile had been a blank at first, with power to shape some picture on its surface from the disjointed fragments of his thoughts, there would have been a copy of old Marley's head on every one.

"Humbug!" said Scrooge; and walked across the room.

After several turns, he sat down again. As he threw his head back in the chair, his glance happened to rest upon a bell, a disused bell, that hung in the room, and communicated for some purpose now forgotten with a chamber in the highest story of the building. It was with great astonishment, and with a strange, inexplicable dread, that as he looked, he saw this bell begin to swing. It swung so softly in the outset that it scarcely made a sound; but soon it rang out loudly, and so did every bell in the house.

With surprising speed, he reached out and grabbed the dagger, pulling it close to his side. He lowered the tip so that it pointed ahead towards the direction of the sound.

This might have lasted half a minute, or a minute, but it seemed an hour. The bells ceased as they had begun, together. They were succeeded by a clanking noise, deep down below; as if some person were dragging a heavy chain over the casks in the wine-merchant's cellar. Scrooge then remembered to have heard that ghosts in haunted houses were described as dragging chains.

The cellar-door flew open with a booming sound, and then he heard the noise much louder, on the floors below; then coming up the stairs; then coming straight towards his door.

He held the dagger out in front of him, the thoughts of his last battles with the undead racing to the top of his mind. If nothing else, Scrooge refused to suffer the same face as Marley had when dragged down and eaten alive by those vile things.

"Could it be that they have come back and they want to finish me like they did Marley?" asked Scrooge to himself.

He looked around the room for any others weapons, cursing himself for leaving his old sword back out of the room. As he scanned the darkness of the room, his anger and then disbelief returned. He scowled as he turned back to the direction of the sound.

"It's humbug still!" said Scrooge. "I won't believe it. We killed them all in the end, every last one of them!"

His colour changed though, when, without a pause, it came on through the heavy door, and passed into the room before his eyes. Upon its coming in, the dying flame leaped up, as though it cried, "I know him; Marley's Ghost!" and fell again.

MARLEY'S GHOST

The same face: the very same. Marley in his pigtail, usual waistcoat, tights and boots; the tassels on the latter bristling, like his pigtail, and his coat-skirts, and the hair upon his head. He still carried the wounds he had sustained during his struggle and death, but apart from that he was the vision of the man he once knew.

The chain he drew was clasped about his middle. It was long, and wound about him like a tail; and it was made (for Scrooge observed it closely) of cash-boxes, keys, padlocks, ledgers, deeds, and heavy purses wrought in steel. His body was transparent; so that Scrooge, observing him, and looking through his waistcoat, could see the two buttons on his coat behind.

Around his waist, he carried a sword belt of some kind

that Scrooge vaguely recognised.

Scrooge had often heard it said that Marley had no bowels, but he had never believed it until now.

No, nor did he believe it even now. Though he looked the phantom through and through, and saw it standing before him; though he felt the chilling influence of its death-cold eyes; and marked the very texture of the folded kerchief bound about its head and chin, which wrapper he had not observed before; he was still incredulous, and fought against his senses.

"How now!" said Scrooge, caustic and cold as ever. "What do you want with me?"

"Much!"—Marley's voice, no doubt about it.

"Who are you?"

"Ask me who I was."

"Who were you then?" said Scrooge, raising his voice. "You're particular, for a shade." He was going to say "to a shade," but substituted this, as more appropriate.

"In life I was your partner, Jacob Marley."

"Can you—can you sit down?" asked Scrooge, looking doubtfully at him.

"I can."

"Do it, then."

Scrooge asked the question, because he didn't know whether a ghost so transparent might find himself in a condition to take a chair; and felt that in the event of its being impossible, it might involve the necessity of an embarrassing explanation. But the ghost sat down on the opposite side of the fireplace, as if he were quite used to it.

"You don't believe in me," observed the Ghost.

"I don't," said Scrooge.

"What evidence would you have of my reality beyond that of your senses?"

"I don't know," said Scrooge.

"Why do you doubt your senses?"

"Because," said Scrooge, "a little thing affects them. A slight disorder of the stomach makes them cheats. You may be an undigested bit of beef, a blot of mustard, a crumb of cheese, a fragment of an underdone potato. There's more of gravy than of grave about you, whatever you are!"

Scrooge was not much in the habit of cracking jokes, nor did he feel, in his heart, by any means waggish then. The truth is, that he tried to be smart, as a means of distracting his own attention, and keeping down his terror; for the spectre's voice disturbed the very marrow in his bones.

"In the past I have dreamt of all kinds of curiosities but not once have I seen you in such a manner," he said whilst taking a step back.

He thought to himself and then came to the simple realisation that he must be feeling unwell and the reason for seeing this vision of old Marley was because of the visit earlier that day by the gentlemen. He looked up to the Spirit though and his doubt returned. It appeared real enough and it certainly sent a chill of fear down his back of the kind he had not felt since his short time in the militia or even worse, the few minutes he spent fighting the undead seven years ago.

To sit, staring at those fixed glazed eyes, in silence for a moment, would play, Scrooge felt, the very deuce with him. There was something very awful, too, in the spectre's being provided with an infernal atmosphere of its own. Scrooge could not feel it himself, but this was clearly the case; for though the Ghost sat perfectly motionless, its hair, and skirts, and tassels, were still agitated as by the hot vapour from an oven.

"You see this toothpick?" said Scrooge, returning quickly to the charge, for the reason just assigned; and wishing, though it were only for a second, to divert the vision's stony gaze from himself.

"I do," replied the Ghost.

"You are not looking at it," said Scrooge.

"But I see it," said the Ghost, "notwithstanding."

"Well!" returned Scrooge, "I have but to swallow this, and be for the rest of my days persecuted by a legion of goblins, all of my own creation. Humbug, I tell you! humbug!"

At this the spirit raised a frightful cry, and shook its chain with such a dismal and appalling noise, that Scrooge held on tight to his chair, to save himself from falling in a swoon. He dropped his dagger with the fear of the ghostly apparition ahead of him, before he was able to strengthen his resolve and issue one final challenge to the ghostly figure.

"You could be a simple illusion, one based upon the science of light and glass. Nothing you have told me was of secret to anybody else. Why, you could be one of my competitors trying to steal custom and trade from my very person, perhaps by using some foul poison or drug," he said with a look of triumphalism to his face.

The Spirit appeared more agitated, crying out in anger and bitterness towards Scrooge but this was not enough, Scrooge was now convinced, deep in his mind that the Spirit was a way of driving him mad or to do something to compromise himself and his business.

"I do not have much time, you should not waste it with your arguments," he said with effort.

"If you are truly Marley, then tell me something that only you and I do know and not some simple business transaction. Tell me, what happened on the night of your death?" asked Scrooge with a look of mischief in his eye.

"Scrooge, you know too well what happened on that night. I am here for the very reason that you too will soon join me on that path!" it cried.

"Humbug! You tell me nothing new, sir, other than to try and stop my commerce," he answered with the sound of accomplishment to his voice.

Scrooge looked around the room, presumably looking for a third party or something that helped to control the creature yet saw nothing that could create the fearsome apparition in his very home. He thought for a brief moment of those people that could have gained access to his house and might bear him ill will. "But why would they want to punish me?" he asked himself.

Scrooge turned his gaze back to the Spirit, looking for answers but before he could speak the Spirit opened is jaw and spoke quickly, as though the very time it had remaining were just a few brief seconds.

"Seven years ago you and I, two men with a history of financial prudence and success, were at the centre of the greatest calamity this city has ever seen. Even our short time in the Yeomanry was nothing compared to the horrors we saw that night," it said as it looked closely at Scrooge.

"Do you remember why we were at the Bank that day?" asked Marley.

"Why do you not tell me if you are so familiar with our history?" Scrooge smirked.

The Spirit looked angry at first and started to move towards Scrooge. It then paused and appeared to be considering the situation. In a far more terrifying turn, it simply grinned in a sinister fashion before continuing and this more than anything terrified Scrooge.

"Money, my dear Scrooge, money," he said with a sad laugh.

"We were already near the Bank having completed our transaction a few moments before. As we left, we saw the first of the walking dead enter the street. Do you remember them Ebenezer?" he asked.

Scrooge nodded as he lowered his head though it was hard to tell if it was out of deference, fear or shame. In Scrooge's case, it could have been all three!

"The Yeomanry cleared the road quite quickly and the survivors, for want of a better word, were chased and cut down as they tried to disappear into the dark alleys of London. This was nothing however compared to the march on the Bank."

"Yes, the Bank, I remember it," said Scrooge as the memories of the day appeared in his mind.

"Though we had seen the first part of the attacks in the city we chose to not help. Maybe we were right to do so. The militia did as fine a job as we could ever have done. It was not long afterwards that the sea of undead arrived. This time it wasn't a few score, it was a myriad, thousands of them and even as the young, the feeble and the helpless were consumed by the walking dead we chose to rush back to the Bank to protect our funds from the looters and the dead," said Marley as he stared intently as Scrooge.

The ghostly apparition adjusted his position pulled on one of the many boxes chained to him. One of them bore the marks of the Bank itself.

"Yes, of course. That is no secret though. We had deposited substantial funds earlier that day and there was a strong, no, a certainty that the calamity to fall upon London would result on a possible loss of our equity still held at the Bank," said Scrooge.

"But of course that was not why I died and you lived that day, was it?"

"Go on, if you truly known what happened, tell me. How did you die Mr. Marley?" he cried out, half expecting another groan from the shade.

"My time is limited Ebenezer and I am here to give you a final chance to avoid my fate. I will say this only once so listen and listen well. The National Provincial Bank was already being ransacked by undesirables when we arrived. If you recall we forced our way inside using our sticks with great effectiveness. Once inside we found the workless and poor busy taking what we considered the fruits of our labours," he said.

"Yes, that is true and what a ghastly sight it was too," answered Scrooge.

"Ghastly? These poor wretches were simply trying to take something before the monstrous horde overwhelmed the whole of the city. Many of them had already lost family members as they tried to escape and just need a little money to buy food and clothing."

"Overwhelmed? Humbug! If you remember, the

Yeomanry arrived in short notice and after a bloody and rather decisive battle were able to halt their progress and stop the attack. This was merely an excuse for the wretched and lazy to steal from others the things they were unwilling to earn for themselves!"

"I do not have long old friend. It is simple. You and I were both inside the Bank when the looters rushed in. We fought them off with our sticks and were doing a damned good job until the creatures entered. They came inside and that is when we saw the box."

"Yes the box, you remember it?" asked Scrooge.

"Of course, it is the box that was my final downfall," said the Spirit.

"We fought them for a long time, even when the soldiers arrived we fought until we were able to reach one of the doors. The fight was still going on when I ran back to pick up the box."

The creature turned its head to reveal a scar on its temple. "This is where I was struck," he said.

Scrooge stepped closer though he was suspicious of the Spirit and its motives. He could see the injury it was pointing to and it certainly appeared to be in the same place that he was struck, though it was a good number of years ago now.

"You ran Ebenezer, and those things did their work. I was unconscious so I never saw what they did but these scars remind me about what happened," he said accusingly.

"There was nothing I could do," muttered Scrooge as he stepped backwards.

"The Bank was overrun and those undead beasts were biting and killing all around us. We should have left but you chose to go back for the box. I saw them strike you and they ran from the Bank. I don't know to this day if the Army caught them or not," he said before looking back at the Spirit.

"What of the box? If you know so much, tell me the whereabouts of that box?"

"Ah, indeed. The box is not important it is what is inside. The artefact holds a terrible secret and we, no, you were lucky that day. If the artefact should ever reach the basement of that Bank," he said wolfishly.

"What? What will happen?" begged Scrooge.

The Spirit said nothing; it simply stared at Scrooge whilst the frightened man attempted to regain his composure.

"I could still be dreaming you wretched thing. I do not believe you, not one word! You are trying to scare me with parlour tricks and lies!" cried Scrooge, though the tone in his voice suggested otherwise.

But how much greater was his horror, when the phantom taking off the bandage round its head, as if it were too warm to wear indoors, its lower jaw dropped down upon its breast like the jaw from mighty monster of ancient myth.

For a moment Scrooge thought he might be standing in front of the walking dead once more, the hanging limbs, sagging jaw were all signs of the creatures he had already seen. This one however was with sinister purpose and terrifying in ways that the undead never were. Unlike the walking dead, this deathly thing seemed to be focusing all of its malevolent attention onto him.

Scrooge fell upon his knees, and clasped his hands before his face.

"Mercy!" he said. "Dreadful apparition, why do you trouble me?"

"Man of the worldly mind!" replied the Ghost, "do you believe in me or not?"

"I do," said Scrooge. "I must. But why do spirits walk the earth, and why do they come to me? I know I am a successful businessman and that my very endeavours already help many through our well funded institutions. Why then are ghostly visions coming to see me in particular? I am to experience a particularly significant or valuable fate that demands warning?" he asked.

The Spirit looked surprised for a moment, perhaps thinking that Scrooge may understand more than he expected before realising that his words were simply repeating his own high opinions of himself and his business dealings.

"It is required of every man," the Ghost returned, "that the spirit within him should walk abroad among his fellowmen, and travel far and wide; and if that spirit goes not forth in life, it is condemned to do so after death. It is doomed to wander through the world—oh, woe is me!—and witness what it cannot share, but might have shared on earth, and turned to happiness!"

"Your argument makes no sense, man. You suggest that as a punishment for not being frivolous with money, and not travelling enough, we must be punished in death with these anchors of metal? That is balderdash, sir! So if I travelled far and wide, as a sailor might, then I am doomed to an eternity of doing nothing? By your definition I already have the better of the options."

Again the spectre raised a cry, and shook its chain and wrung its shadowy hands.

"You are fettered," said Scrooge, trembling. "Tell me why? Are you here for your sins or to complain about the hard work that I do and the good I bring this world through my successes?" he demanded.

"I wear the chain I forged in life," replied the Ghost. "I made it link by link, and yard by yard; I girded it on of my own free will, and of my own free will I wore it. Look at it! Look at the fine work and effort that has gone into its creation. Is its pattern strange to you?"

Scrooge trembled more and more.

"Or would you know," pursued the Ghost, "the weight and length of the strong coil you bear yourself? It was full as heavy and as long as this, seven Christmas Eves ago.

You have laboured on it, since. It is a ponderous chain!"

Scrooge glanced about him on the floor, in the expectation of finding himself surrounded by some fifty or sixty fathoms of iron cable: but he could see nothing. He looked back at the Spirit, examining the chain once more and noticing the many artefacts, chests, padlocks and coils that held it together. It reminded him of the description of the Gorgon's with their twisted hair made of writhing, tangled snakes.

"I don't understand. You died, not because of money. You were simply overpowered by those foul, unbreathing monsters and killed before my very eyes and yet say you are being punished for having been a good businessman. I cannot see what you have done wrong and yet you suggest my fate is the same or worse than your own," said Scrooge in an almost impassioned plea.

"Jacob," he said, imploringly. "Old Jacob Marley, tell me more. Speak comfort to me, Jacob!"

"I have none to give," the Ghost replied. "It comes from other regions, Ebenezer Scrooge, and is conveyed by other ministers, to other kinds of men. Nor can I tell you what I would. A very little more is all permitted to me. I cannot rest, I cannot stay, I cannot linger anywhere. My spirit never walked beyond our counting-house—mark me!—in life my spirit never roved beyond the narrow limits of our money-changing hole; and weary journeys lie before me!"

It was a habit with Scrooge, whenever he became thoughtful, to put his hands in his breeches pockets. Pondering on what the Ghost had said, he did so now, but without lifting up his eyes, or getting off his knees.

"You must have been very slow about it, Jacob," Scrooge observed, in a business-like manner, though with humility and deference.

"Slow!" the Ghost repeated.

"Seven years dead," mused Scrooge. "And travelling all the time!"

"The whole time," said the Ghost. "No rest, no peace. Incessant torture of remorse."

"You travel fast?" said Scrooge.

"On the wings of the wind," replied the Ghost.

"You might have got over a great quantity of ground in seven years," said Scrooge.

The Ghost, on hearing this, set up another cry, and clanked its chain so hideously in the dead silence of the night, that the Ward would have been justified in indicting it for a nuisance.

"Oh! captive, bound, and double-ironed," cried the phantom, "not to know, that ages of incessant labour by immortal creatures, for this earth must pass into eternity before the good of which it is susceptible is all developed. Not to know that any Christian spirit working kindly in its little sphere, whatever it may be, will find its mortal life too short for its vast means of usefulness. Not to know that no space of regret can make amends for one life's opportunity misused! Yet such was I! Oh! such was I!"

"But you were always a good man of business, Jacob," faltered Scrooge, who now began to apply this to himself.

"Business!" cried the Ghost, wringing its hands again. "Mankind was my business. The common welfare was my business; charity, mercy, forbearance, and benevolence, were, all, my business. The dealings of my trade were but a drop of water in the comprehensive ocean of my business!"

It held up its chain at arm's length, as if that were the cause of all its unavailing grief, and flung it heavily upon the ground again.

"At this time of the rolling year," the spectre said, "I suffer most. Why did I walk through crowds of fellow-beings with my eyes turned down, and never raise them to that blessed Star which led the Wise Men to a poor abode! Were there no poor homes to which its light would have conducted me!"

Scrooge was very much dismayed to hear the spectre going on at this rate, and began to quake exceedingly.

"Hear me!" cried the Ghost. "My time is nearly gone."

"I will," said Scrooge. "But don't be hard upon me! Don't be flowery, Jacob! Pray!"

"How it is that I appear before you in a shape that you can see, I may not tell. I have sat invisible beside you many and many a day."

It was not an agreeable idea. Scrooge shivered, and wiped the perspiration from his brow.

"That is no light part of my penance," pursued the Ghost. "I am here to-night to warn you, that you have yet a chance and hope of escaping my fate. A chance and hope of my procuring, Ebenezer."

"You were always a good friend to me," said Scrooge. "Thank'ee!"

"You will be haunted," resumed the Ghost, "by Three Spirits."

Scrooge's countenance fell almost as low as the Ghost's had done.

"Is that the chance and hope you mentioned, Jacob?" he demanded, in a faltering voice.

"It is."

"I—I think I'd rather not," said Scrooge.

"Without their visits," said the Ghost, "you cannot hope to shun the path I tread. Your fate and that of the good people of this city rely upon what you do in the next day. It was my fate to turn from those around me for nothing more than personal gain. If I had held even the smallest spark of compassion then I would not be roaming this place. Listen to them Ebenezer, listen to them well for they will show you all you need to see. Expect the first to-morrow, when the bell tolls One."

"Couldn't I take 'em all at once, and have it over, Jacob?" hinted Scrooge.

"Expect the second on the next night at the same hour. The third upon the next night when the last stroke of Twelve has ceased to vibrate. Look to see me no more; and look that, for your own sake, you remember what has passed between us!"

When it had said these words, the spectre took its wrapper from the table, and bound it round its head, as before. Scrooge knew this, by the smart sound its teeth made, when the jaws were brought together by the bandage. He ventured to raise his eyes again, and found his supernatural visitor confronting him in an erect attitude, with its chain wound over and about its arm.

The apparition walked backward from him; and at every step it took, the window raised itself a little, so that when the spectre reached it, it was wide open.

It beckoned Scrooge to approach, which he did. When they were within two paces of each other, Marley's Ghost held up its hand, warning him to come no nearer. Scrooge stopped.

Not so much in obedience, as in surprise and fear: for on the raising of the hand, he became sensible of confused noises in the air; incoherent sounds of lamentation and regret; wailings inexpressibly sorrowful and self-accusatory. The spectre, after listening for a moment, joined in the mournful dirge; and floated out upon the bleak, dark night.

Scrooge followed to the window: desperate in his

curiosity. He looked out.

The air was filled with phantoms, wandering hither and thither in restless haste, and moaning as they went. Every one of them wore chains like Marley's Ghost; some few (they might be guilty governments) were linked together; none were free. Many had been personally known to Scrooge in their lives. He had been quite familiar with one old ghost, in a white waistcoat, with a monstrous iron safe attached to its ankle, who cried piteously at being unable to assist a wretched woman with an infant, whom it saw below, upon a door-step. The misery with them all was, clearly, that they sought to interfere, for good, in human matters, and had lost the power for ever.

Whether these creatures faded into mist, or mist enshrouded them, he could not tell. But they and their spirit voices faded together; and the night became as it had been when he walked home. He paused for a moment, feeling sure he could hear wailing or screams but the sound of the wind swept in until he was convinced it must have been part of the awful apparition.

"Could old Jacob be right? Was his soul truly damned because he had stuck to such a fastidious path as finance and self-responsibility? Could he have been saved if one of them had turned from the Bank rather than running back for more?"

Scrooge continued looking for signs of trouble but the city had returned to its normal state, though Scrooge still muttered to himself as he considered the words of his old friend.

He sighed and then closed the window, and examined the door by which the Ghost had entered. It was double-locked, as he had locked it with his own hands, and the bolts were undisturbed. He tried to say "Humbug!" but stopped at the first syllable. And being, from the emotion he had undergone, or the fatigues of the day, or his glimpse of the Invisible World, or the dull conversation of the Ghost, or the lateness of the hour, much in need of repose; went straight to bed, without undressing, and fell asleep upon the instant.

STAVE TWO

THE FIRST OF THE THREE SPIRITS.

When Scrooge awoke, it was so dark, that looking out of bed, he could scarcely distinguish the transparent window from the opaque walls of his chamber. He was endeavouring to pierce the darkness with his ferret eyes, when the chimes of a neighbouring church struck the four quarters. So he listened for the hour.

He was quite familiar with the clock and used it to assist in his daily time keeping. As the familiarity of the sounds calmed him, he listened intently for the subsequent chimes. He half expected some kind of phantom terror to tear open his door or to crash through the window at the sound of each chime.

To his great astonishment the heavy bell went on from six to seven, and from seven to eight, and regularly up to twelve; then stopped. Twelve! It was past two when he went to bed. The clock was wrong. An icicle must have got into the works. Twelve!

He touched the spring of his repeater, to correct this most preposterous clock. Its rapid little pulse beat twelve: and stopped.

"Why, it isn't possible," said Scrooge, "that I can have slept through a whole day and far into another night. It isn't possible that anything has happened to the sun, and this is twelve at noon!"

The idea being an alarming one, he scrambled out of bed, and groped his way to the window. He was obliged to rub the frost off with the sleeve of his dressing-gown before he could see anything; and could see very little then. All he could make out was, that it was still very foggy and extremely cold, and that there was no noise of people running to and fro, and making a great stir, as there unquestionably would have been if night had beaten off bright day, and taken possession of the world.

There was noise outside, though to old Scrooge it was the sound of people going about their business. Just a slightly more careful examination would have revealed the first of the plague's victims stumbling through the lanes and into the darkness as the cursed object began its journey towards the heart of the city. The first of its victims were already starting their dark journey that began with sickness and fever and then moved on into pain, weakness and then coma. As the pulse slowed and the life drained the victim would die. In some it could be days, in the weaker, it could be mere hours before death took them. No matter their resilience though, once dead the transformation was fast and always successful.

Scrooge listened again and could hear nothing that should trouble him unduly, for now, this was a great relief, because "three days after sight of this First of Exchange pay to Mr. Ebenezer Scrooge or his order," and so forth, would have become a mere United States' security if there were no days to count by.

Scrooge went to bed again, and thought, and thought, and thought it over and over and over, and could make nothing of it. The more he thought, the more perplexed he was; and the more he endeavoured not to think, the more he thought. Every few moments he was able to empty his mind and he did his utmost to concentrate on nothing but nothingness. All it took though was but a single thought or memory and the entire affair expanded before his eyes. As soon as the memories filled his mind, he knew he would be able to do nothing other than to dwell upon the awfulness of them.

Marley's Ghost bothered him exceedingly. Every time he resolved within himself, after mature inquiry, that it was all a dream, his mind flew back again, like a strong spring released, to its first position, and presented the same problem to be worked all through, "Was it a dream or not?"

The matter of the death of Marley weighed heavily with Scrooge. It was an event that he rarely considered and yet the event that had taken the closest person to Scrooge. The day was one of those terrible life-changing moments when all his beliefs and fears were transformed by the mythical dead wandering the streets. Worse than the death though was the manner in which Marley had died. "Perhaps the dreams were caused by him noticing something in the day that reminded him of the awful violence and death that had occurred in London that day?" he thought.

Scrooge lay there, his mind wandering and doing its best to persuade him that the events concerning Marley's death were in fact far less dramatic and that it was simply his overactive imagination that had furnished them with such impossible things. Just as he made the decision that this was so, a chill spread in his chest as though a pistol's flint had been cocked next to his head, and the dreaded fear returned to his heart. It was the fear of a man that had awoken from a dream only to find the world of the living was the hell and the world of dream was the one of peace and serenity.

Scrooge lay in this state until the chime had gone three quarters more, when he remembered, on a sudden, that the Ghost had warned him of a visitation when the bell tolled one. He resolved to lie awake until the hour was passed; and, considering that he could no more go to sleep than go to Heaven, this was perhaps the wisest resolution in his power.

The quarter was so long, that he was more than once convinced he must have sunk into a doze unconsciously, and missed the clock. At length it broke upon his listening ear.

"Ding, dong!"

"A quarter past," said Scrooge, counting.

"Ding, dong!"

"Half-past!" said Scrooge.

"Ding, dong!"

"A quarter to it," said Scrooge.

"Ding, dong!"

"The hour itself," said Scrooge, triumphantly, "and nothing else!"

He spoke before the hour bell sounded, which it now did with a deep, dull, hollow, melancholy One. Light flashed up in the room upon the instant, and the curtains of his bed were drawn.

The curtains of his bed were drawn aside, I tell you, by a hand. Not the curtains at his feet, nor the curtains at his back, but those to which his face was addressed. The curtains of his bed were drawn aside; and Scrooge, starting up into a half-recumbent attitude, found himself face to face with the unearthly visitor who drew them: as close to it as I am now to you, and I am standing in the spirit at your elbow.

For a moment, he considered grabbing the weapons he had now pulled near his bed in case of being faced with a deadly, ethereal foe but there was something about this Spirit that was both fearsome and friendly. Something deep inside him told him that this creature was there for a common purpose, not to harm him. His mind tried to calm him yet his heart, still trembling from his dreams, troubled him and pounded like an anvil in his chest.

It was a strange figure—like a child: yet not so like a child as like an old man, viewed through some supernatural medium, which gave him the appearance of having receded from the view, and being diminished to a child's proportions. Its hair, which hung about its neck and down its back, was white as if with age; and yet the face had not a wrinkle in it, and the tenderest bloom was on the skin. Its body reminded him of the classical sculptures of the great heroes of Ancient Greece. The rippling muscles of Achilles and the brute strength of Herakles.

The arms were very long and muscular; the hands the same, as if its hold were of uncommon strength. Scrooge could easily image it swinging a mighty club or pulling down wild beast with nothing but brute strength. Its legs and feet, most delicately formed, were, like those upper members, bare. It wore a tunic of the purest white; and round its waist was bound a lustrous belt, the sheen of which was beautiful. It held a branch of fresh green holly in its hand; and, in singular contradiction of that wintry emblem, had its dress trimmed with summer flowers. But the strangest thing about it was, that from the crown of its head there sprung a bright clear jet of light, by which all this was visible; and which was doubtless the occasion of its using, in its duller moments, a great extinguisher for a cap, which it now held under its arm.

Even this, though, when Scrooge looked at it with increasing steadiness, was not its strangest quality. For as its belt sparkled and glittered now in one part and now in another, and what was light one instant, at another time was dark, so the figure itself fluctuated in its distinctness: being now a thing with one arm, now with one leg, now with twenty legs, now a pair of legs without a head, now a head without a body: of which dissolving parts, no outline would be visible in the dense gloom wherein they melted away. And in the very wonder of this, it would be itself again; distinct and clear as ever.

"Are you the Spirit, sir, whose coming was foretold to me?" asked Scrooge.

"I am!"

The voice was soft and gentle. Singularly low, as if instead of being so close beside him, it were at a distance.

"Who, and what are you?" Scrooge demanded.

"I am the Ghost of Christmas Past."

"Long Past?" inquired Scrooge: observant of its dwarfish stature.

"No. Your past."

Perhaps, Scrooge could not have told anybody why, if anybody could have asked him; but he had a special desire to see the Spirit in his cap; and begged him to be covered.

"What!" exclaimed the Ghost, "would you so soon put out, with worldly hands, the light I give? Is it not enough that you are one of those whose passions made this cap, and force me through whole trains of years to wear it low upon my brow!"

Scrooge reverently disclaimed all intention to offend or any knowledge of having wilfully "bonneted" the Spirit at any period of his life. He then made bold to inquire what business brought him there.

"Your welfare!" said the Ghost, "and with it the welfare of this good city," it said as it spread out its arms.

"There are things more important than your own purse, Scrooge. You have seen the Spirits dragging themselves away from here. Why do you think they are leaving? They do not travel for reasons that are minor in nature. Something evil and terrible is coming and it is something you have seen before! It is not far away now and some are already feeling its icy fingers," it said mysteriously.

Scrooge expressed himself much obliged, but could not help thinking that a night of unbroken rest would have been more conducive to that end. The Spirit must have heard him thinking, for it said immediately:

"Your reclamation, then. Take heed!"

It put out its strong hand as it spoke, and clasped him gently by the arm.

"Rise! and walk with me!"

It would have been in vain for Scrooge to plead that the weather and the hour were not adapted to pedestrian purposes; that bed was warm, and the thermometer a long way below freezing; that he was clad but lightly in his slippers, dressing-gown, and nightcap; and that he had a cold upon him at that time. The grasp, though gentle as a woman's hand, was not to be resisted. He rose: but finding that the Spirit made towards the window, clasped his robe in supplication.

"I am a mortal," Scrooge remonstrated, "and liable to fall."

"Bear but a touch of my hand there," said the Spirit, laying it upon his heart, "and you shall be upheld in more than this!"

As the words were spoken, they passed through the wall, and stood upon an open country road, with fields on either hand. The city had entirely vanished. Not a vestige of it was to be seen. The darkness and the mist had vanished with it, for it was a clear, cold, winter day, with snow upon the ground.

"Good Heaven!" said Scrooge, clasping his hands together, as he looked about him. "I was bred in this place. I was a boy here!"

The Spirit gazed upon him mildly. Its gentle touch,

though it had been light and instantaneous, appeared still present to the old man's sense of feeling. He was conscious of a thousand odours floating in the air, each one connected with a thousand thoughts, and hopes, and joys, and cares long, long, forgotten!

"Your lip is trembling," said the Ghost. "And what is that upon your cheek?"

Scrooge muttered, with an unusual catching in his voice, that it was a pimple; and begged the Ghost to lead him where he would.

"You recollect the way?" inquired the Spirit.

"Remember it!" cried Scrooge with fervour; "I could walk it blindfold."

"Strange to have forgotten it for so many years!" observed the Ghost. "Let us go on."

They walked along the road, Scrooge recognising every gate, and post, and tree; until a little market-town appeared in the distance, with its bridge, its church, and winding river. Some shaggy ponies now were seen trotting towards them with boys upon their backs, who called to other boys in country gigs and carts, driven by farmers. All these boys were in great spirits, and shouted to each other, until the broad fields were so full of merry music, that the crisp air laughed to hear it!

"These are but shadows of the things that have been," said the Ghost. "They have no consciousness of us."

The jocund travellers came on; and as they came,

Scrooge knew and named them every one. Why was he rejoiced beyond all bounds to see them! Why did his cold eye glisten, and his heart leap up as they went past! Why was he filled with gladness when he heard them give each other Merry Christmas, as they parted at cross-roads and bye-ways, for their several homes!

A group of yeoman cavalry, resplendent in their bright uniforms rode gently past, the boys jumping and waving at them as the gallant soldiers moved on and through the road.

What was merry Christmas to Scrooge? Out upon merry Christmas! What good had it ever done to him?

"The school is not quite deserted," said the Ghost. "A solitary child, neglected by his friends, is left there still."

Scrooge said he knew it. And he sobbed.

They left the high-road, by a well-remembered lane, and soon approached a mansion of dull red brick, with a little weathercock-surmounted cupola, on the roof, and a bell hanging in it. It was a large house, but one of broken fortunes; for the spacious offices were little used, their walls were damp and mossy, their windows broken, and their gates decayed. Fowls clucked and strutted in the stables; and the coach-houses and sheds were over-run with grass. Nor was it more retentive of its ancient state, within; for entering the dreary hall, and glancing through the open doors of many rooms, they found them poorly furnished, cold, and vast. There was an earthy savour in the air, a chilly bareness in the place, which associated itself somehow with too much getting up by candle-light, and not too much to eat.

As they entered, Scrooge held back. The darkness and coolness of the place reminding him of something he had long forgotten. The Spirit looked to him and back to where they were to travel. Scrooge took a deep breath and with a great effort pushed on.

They went, the Ghost and Scrooge, across the hall, to a door at the back of the house. It opened before them, and disclosed a long, bare, melancholy room, made barer still by lines of plain deal forms and desks. At one of these a lonely boy was reading near a feeble fire; and Scrooge sat down upon a form, and wept to see his poor forgotten self as he used to be.

Not a latent echo in the house, not a squeak and scuffle from the mice behind the panelling, not a drip from the half-thawed water-spout in the dull yard behind, not a sigh among the leafless boughs of one despondent poplar, not the idle swinging of an empty store-house door, no, not a clicking in the fire, but fell upon the heart of Scrooge with a softening influence, and gave a freer passage to his tears.

The Spirit touched him on the arm, and pointed to his younger self, intent upon his reading. Suddenly a man, in foreign garments: wonderfully real and distinct to look at: stood outside the window, with an axe stuck in his belt, and leading by the bridle an ass laden with wood.

"Why, it's Ali Baba!" Scrooge exclaimed in ecstasy. "It's dear old honest Ali Baba! Yes, yes, I know! One Christmas time, when yonder solitary child was left here all alone, he did come, for the first time, just like that. Poor boy! And Valentine," said Scrooge, "and his wild brother, Orson; there they go! And what's his name, who was put down in his drawers, asleep, at the Gate of Damascus; don't you see him! And the Sultan's Groom turned upside down by the Genii; there he is upon his head! Serve him right. I'm glad of it. What business had he to be married to the Princess!"

To hear Scrooge expending all the earnestness of his nature on such subjects, in a most extraordinary voice between laughing and crying; and to see his heightened and excited face; would have been a surprise to his business friends in the city, indeed.

"There's the Parrot!" cried Scrooge. "Green body and yellow tail, with a thing like a lettuce growing out of the top of his head; there he is! Poor Robin Crusoe, he called him, when he came home again after sailing round the island. 'Poor Robin Crusoe, where have you been, Robin Crusoe?' The man thought he was dreaming, but he wasn't. It was the Parrot, you know. There goes Friday, running for his life to the little creek! Halloa! Hoop! Halloo!"

Then, with a rapidity of transition very foreign to his usual character, he said, in pity for his former self, "Poor boy!" and cried again.

"I wish," Scrooge muttered, putting his hand in his

pocket, and looking about him, after drying his eyes with his cuff: "but it's too late now."

"What is the matter?" asked the Spirit.

"Nothing," said Scrooge. "Nothing. There was a boy singing a Christmas Carol at my door last night. I should like to have given him something: that's all."

The Ghost smiled thoughtfully, and waved its hand: saying as it did so, "Let us see another Christmas!"

Scrooge's former self grew larger at the words, and the room became a little darker and more dirty. The panels shrunk, the windows cracked; fragments of plaster fell out of the ceiling, and the naked laths were shown instead; but how all this was brought about, Scrooge knew no more than you do. He only knew that it was quite correct; that everything had happened so; that there he was, alone again, when all the other boys had gone home for the jolly holidays.

He was not reading now, but walking up and down despairingly. Scrooge looked at the Ghost, and with a mournful shaking of his head, glanced anxiously towards the door.

It opened; and a little girl, much younger than the boy, came darting in, and putting her arms about his neck, and often kissing him, addressed him as her "Dear, dear brother."

"I have come to bring you home, dear brother!" said the child, clapping her tiny hands, and bending down to laugh. "To bring you home, home, home!"

"Home, little Fan?" returned the boy.

"Yes!" said the child, brimful of glee. "Home, for good and all. Home, for ever and ever. Father is so much kinder than he used to be, that home's like Heaven! He spoke so gently to me one dear night when I was going to bed, that I was not afraid to ask him once more if you might come home; and he said Yes, you should; and sent me in a coach to bring you. And you're to be a man!" said the child, opening her eyes, "and are never to come back here; but first, we're to be together all the Christmas long, and have the merriest time in all the world."

"You are quite a woman, little Fan!" exclaimed the boy.

She clapped her hands and laughed, and tried to touch his head; but being too little, laughed again, and stood on tiptoe to embrace him. Then she began to drag him, in her childish eagerness, towards the door; and he, nothing loth to go, accompanied her.

A terrible voice in the hall cried, "Bring down Master Scrooge's box, there!" and in the hall appeared the schoolmaster himself, who glared on Master Scrooge with a ferocious condescension, and threw him into a dreadful state of mind by shaking hands with him. He then conveyed him and his sister into the veriest old well of a shivering best-parlour that ever was seen, where the maps upon the wall, and the celestial and terrestrial globes in the windows, were waxy with cold. Here he produced a decanter of curiously light wine, and a block of curiously heavy cake, and administered instalments of those dainties to the young people: at the same time, sending out a meagre servant to offer a glass of "something" to the postboy, who answered that he thanked the gentleman, but if it was the same tap as he had tasted before, he had rather not. Master Scrooge's trunk being by this time tied on to the top of the chaise, the children bade the schoolmaster good-bye right willingly; and getting into it, drove gaily down the garden-sweep: the quick wheels dashing the hoar-frost and snow from off the dark leaves of the evergreens like spray.

"Always a delicate creature, whom a breath might have withered," said the Ghost. "But she had a large heart!"

"So she had," cried Scrooge. "You're right. I will not gainsay it, Spirit. God forbid!"

"She died a woman," said the Ghost, "and had, as I think, children."

"One child," Scrooge returned.

"True," said the Ghost. "Your nephew!"

Scrooge seemed uneasy in his mind; and answered briefly, "Yes."

Although they had but that moment left the school behind them, they were now in the busy thoroughfares of a city, where shadowy passengers passed and repassed; where shadowy carts and coaches battled for the way, and all the strife and tumult of a real city were. It was made plain enough, by the dressing of the shops, that here too it was Christmas time again; but it was evening, and the streets were lighted up.

The Ghost stopped at a certain warehouse door, and asked Scrooge if he knew it.

"Know it!" said Scrooge. "Was I apprenticed here!"

They went in. At sight of an old gentleman in a Welsh wig, sitting behind such a high desk, that if he had been two inches taller he must have knocked his head against the ceiling, Scrooge cried in great excitement:

"Why, it's old Fezziwig! Bless his heart; it's Fezziwig alive again!"

Old Fezziwig laid down his pen, and looked up at the clock, which pointed to the hour of seven. He rubbed his hands; adjusted his capacious waistcoat; laughed all over himself, from his shoes to his organ of benevolence; and called out in a comfortable, oily, rich, fat, jovial voice:

"Yo ho, there! Ebenezer! Dick!"

Scrooge's former self, now grown a young man, came briskly in, accompanied by his fellow-'prentice.

"Dick Wilkins, to be sure!" said Scrooge to the Ghost. "Bless me, yes. There he is. He was very much attached to me, was Dick. Poor Dick! Dear, dear!"

"Yo ho, my boys!" said Fezziwig. "No more work to-night. Christmas Eve, Dick. Christmas, Ebenezer! Let's have the shutters up," cried old Fezziwig, with a sharp clap of his hands, "before a man can say Jack Robinson!"

You wouldn't believe how those two fellows went at it! They charged into the street with the shutters—one, two, three—had 'em up in their places—four, five, six—barred 'em and pinned 'em—seven, eight, nine—and came back before you could have got to twelve, panting like race-horses.

"Hilli-ho!" cried old Fezziwig, skipping down from the high desk, with wonderful agility. "Clear away, my lads, and let's have lots of room here! Hilli-ho, Dick! Chirrup, Ebenezer!"

Clear away! There was nothing they wouldn't have cleared away, or couldn't have cleared away, with old Fezziwig looking on. It was done in a minute. Every movable was packed off, as if it were dismissed from public life for evermore; the floor was swept and watered, the lamps were trimmed, fuel was heaped upon the fire; and the warehouse was as snug, and warm, and dry, and bright a ball-room, as you would desire to see upon a winter's night.

In came a fiddler with a music-book, and went up to the lofty desk, and made an orchestra of it, and tuned like fifty stomach-aches. In came Mrs. Fezziwig, one vast substantial smile. In came the three Miss Fezziwigs, beaming and lovable. In came the six young followers whose hearts they broke. In came all the young men and women employed in the business. In came the housemaid, with her cousin, the baker. In came the cook, with her brother's particular friend, the milkman. In came the boy from over the way, who was suspected of not having board enough from his master; trying to hide himself behind the girl from next door but one, who was proved to have had her ears pulled by her mistress. In they all came, one after another; some shyly, some boldly, some gracefully, some awkwardly, some pushing, some pulling; in they all came, anyhow and everyhow. Away they all went, twenty couple at once; hands half round and back again the other way; down the middle and up again; round and round in various stages of affectionate grouping; old top couple always turning up in the wrong place; new top couple starting off again, as soon as they got there; all top couples at last, and not a bottom one to help them! When this result was brought about, old Fezziwig, clapping his hands to stop the dance, cried out, "Well done!" and the fiddler plunged his hot face into a pot of porter, especially provided for that purpose. But scorning rest, upon his reappearance, he instantly began again, though there were no dancers yet, as if the other fiddler had been carried home, exhausted, on a shutter, and he were a bran-new man resolved to beat him out of sight, or perish.

There were more dances, and there were forfeits, and more dances, and there was cake, and there was negus, and there was a great piece of Cold Roast, and there was a great piece of Cold Boiled, and there were mince-pies, and plenty of beer. But the great effect of the evening came after the Roast and Boiled, when the fiddler (an artful dog, mind! The sort of man who knew his business better than you or I could have told it him!) struck up "Sir Roger de Coverley." Then old Fezziwig stood out to dance with Mrs. Fezziwig. Top couple, too; with a good stiff piece of work cut out for them; three or four and twenty pair of partners; people who were not to be trifled with; people who would dance, and had no notion of walking.

MR. FEZZIWIG'S BALL

But if they had been twice as many—ah, four times—old Fezziwig would have been a match for them, and so would Mrs. Fezziwig. As to her, she was worthy to be his partner in every sense of the term. If that's not high praise, tell me higher, and I'll use it. A positive light appeared to issue from Fezziwig's calves. They shone in every part of the dance like moons. You couldn't have predicted, at any given time, what would have become of them next. And when old Fezziwig and Mrs. Fezziwig had gone all through the dance; advance and retire, both hands to your partner, bow and curtsey, corkscrew, thread-the-needle, and back again to your place; Fezziwig "cut"—cut so deftly, that he appeared to wink with his legs, and came upon his feet again without a stagger.

As the party danced gleefully, a stranger entered from

the darkness outside. He wore a long, scruffy coat and his face hidden in the shadows as he moved closer. Mrs. Fezziwig squealed with excitement as she ran from the dance to embrace the man. The old man looked as though he would be knocked backwards by the tumultuous force of the lady, but he managed to regain his balance after much effort. Separating just a fraction the man pulled down the hood from his coat to reveal the face of a hardened and toughened man. His eyes softened his face, he was immediately recognised by Mr. Fezziwig.

"Mr Jenkins!" he cried in joy as he also moved closely to shake the man.

"What a splendid surprise, we had no idea you were back," he said.

The visitor moved to the side of the room, chatting with the pair whilst the rest of the party continued their dancing.

The Ghost beckoned Scrooge to follow as it moved closer to the little group, allowing them to overhear their discussion. Scrooge raised his hand in protest but the Spirit pulled him with a force that drained his ability to stand away from his legs.

"The regiment has returned to England and I have leave for several weeks and I just had to spend the time to see my sister in this wonderful holiday," explained the man.

"You are always welcome in our home, sir," said Mr.

Fezziwig as he beamed with pleasure.

"Thank you, it is good to be away from the barracks and in the company of civility once more," replied Mr Jenkins with wry grin.

The Ghost turned back to Scrooge, watching him intently as Mr Jenkins explained his recent activity on the continent and the progress of his regiment's campaigns.

"Mr Jenkins was a well-respected officer, when he died his funeral was attended by many, many people. He died with honour and respect."

"I know, I know," said an irate Scrooge, "I read his obituary in the newspaper."

"Yet you failed to attend his funeral even though it was held such a short distance away from your own home," said the Spirit dismissively.

"Did you have no feelings or consideration for this man? Had you never spoken?" he asked, though Scrooge was convinced he already knew the answer.

"Of course I knew him, Mr Jenkins was the man that showed me a sword for the first time," said Scrooge.

As he spoke the room spun and swirled, Scrooge felt he must have been drugged or injured in some frivolous manner. As the walls slowed, he noticed the party was still going on, but he was now off to the side and watching the young Scrooge talking to the old man. It was of course him and Mr Jenkins, the old soldier.

The old man held in front of him a vicious looking

sword, it was dulled and pitted from a hard life in Northern Europe. It reminded Scrooge of the swords he had read about as a young boy in Arabia with its curved blade, much like a scimitar. It certainly looked far from the weapon of an Englishman.

"This is my old friend, my trusty cavalry sabre. We call this the 1796 pattern sword, designed for use by all the light cavalry, including my old regiment. It has served me well these many years. Here, do you want to hold it?" he asked whilst looking at the young man.

The young Scrooge pushed out his hands in excitement towards the weapon and then stopped just before touching the steel. The soldier moved it towards Scrooge and then stopped just shy of a few inches.

"Before you touch it I want you to remember this is a sword of war and not to be trifled with. I have carried that sword in many countries and used it in anger of several occasions. The marks on its blade are from training and war. It is a weapon that deserves your respect."

The young Scrooge nodded, asking but one question. "Is it sharp, sir?"

The soldier laughed loudly as he handed the sheathed sword to Scrooge.

"Indeed it is, though I am told even a dull blade will cut open a Frenchman!" he guffawed.

Scrooge pulled the weapon slowly from its scabbard to reveal its blade and sharp edge. He placed the scabbard to one side and held up the tip towards the wall. Next to Scrooge, the weapon looked large and cumbersome. He lifted it up and tried to swing the weapon but he clumsily moved and nearly embedded it in the floor, much to the amusement of the soldier.

"Good Lord! What has the floor done to you?" laughed Mr. Jenkins as he moved closer.

"Here, let me show you something," he said as he took the sword from his hands.

The soldier held the weapon in front of him with the tip pointing towards Scrooge.

"This sword is designed to be an excellent cutter. There are some that argue that the point and thrusting are the way to fight but you will be hard pressed to use this sword in that manner," he explained, as he made several stabbing motions with the curved sword.

"You see, a good stab may very well kill a man bit it usually won't be right away. A man can still move forwards, and hack and stab at you whilst your sword is stuck impotently inside his body. You will observe the curved blade makes it move and cut quickly and effectively. Watch this," he said, as he proceeded to make a serious of cuts that were so fast in speed and elegant in movement that it almost looked like a dance. As he cut, the sword moved in a series of circles so that the edge was threatening almost continually from many angles.

"If I were on a horse I could strike down like this at

the man's arms or face," he slashed down to one side and then to the other in quick succession.

Scrooge stepped back in astonishment but with a grin that made his mouth look twice as large as it had been just moment before.

The Ghost watched in a form of amusement as the older Mr Scrooge forgot where he was for a moment and moved through a series of cuts whilst holding an imaginary sword. The movements had returned to his mind and in just seconds, the old Scrooge was leaping from side to side as he delivered horizontal and diagonal cuts with his invisible blade. With each cut, his movement became more fluid and relaxed and with it, his cuts became stronger, faster and more accurate. After a full minute of practice, he stopped and looked directly at the Ghost before realising what he had just done.

"Yes?" asked Scrooge, but the Spirit said nothing and simply turned to look back at the room and the dancing.

When Scrooge looked back the old soldier was talking to his sister and the young man was gone, presumably busy dancing with the many others in the room. Scrooge looked through the group of people until he finally spotted his younger self, using a cane in the corner of the room. The young man was practicing almost the exact same movements that the elder Scrooge has been trying just moments before though this Scrooge at least had something physical to swing.

When the clock struck eleven, this domestic ball broke up. Mr. and Mrs. Fezziwig took their stations, one on either side of the door, and shaking hands with every person individually as he or she went out, wished him or her a Merry Christmas. When everybody had retired but the two 'prentices, they did the same to them; and thus the cheerful voices died away, and the lads were left to their beds; which were under a counter in the back-shop.

During the whole of this time, Scrooge had acted like a man out of his wits. His heart and soul were in the scene, and with his former self. He corroborated everything, remembered everything, enjoyed everything, and underwent the strangest agitation. Until today, he had completely forgotten about Mr Jenkins, yet his body obviously retained the memory and skills he had picked up in just those brief moments with the sword. After that event, he had been required to both train with and sometimes to even use a sword but it was this point in time where he had actually touched and held a weapon for the first time. In a way, it was a moment of transition for him and the start of his interest in the weapon. It was not until now, when the bright faces of his former self and Dick were turned from them, that he remembered the Ghost, and became conscious that it was looking full upon him, while the light upon its head burnt very clear.

"A small matter," said the Ghost, "to make these silly folks so full of gratitude."

"Small!" echoed Scrooge.

The Spirit signed to him to listen to the two apprentices, who were pouring out their hearts in praise of Fezziwig: and when he had done so, said,

"Why! Is it not? He has spent but a few pounds of your mortal money: three or four perhaps. Is that so much that he deserves this praise?"

"It isn't that," said Scrooge, heated by the remark, and speaking unconsciously like his former, not his latter, self. "It isn't that, Spirit. He has the power to render us happy or unhappy; to make our service light or burdensome; a pleasure or a toil. Say that his power lies in words and looks; in things so slight and insignificant that it is impossible to add and count 'em up: what then? Even Mr Jenkins, the older soldier was able to spread interest and enjoyment at nothing else other than showing off a few moves with his sword. None of this would be possible without the effort and intention of Fezziwig. The happiness he gives, is quite as great as if it cost a fortune and yet, look at the joy the sight of Mrs. Fezziwig being able to enjoy the company of her brother at this time."

He felt the Spirit's glance, and stopped.

"What is the matter?" asked the Ghost.

"Nothing particular," said Scrooge.

"Something, I think?" the Ghost insisted.

"No," said Scrooge, "No. I should like to be able to say a word or two to my clerk just now. That's all."

His former self turned down the lamps as he gave utterance to the wish; and Scrooge and the Ghost again stood side by side in the open air.

"My time grows short," observed the Spirit. "Quick!"

This was not addressed to Scrooge, or to any one whom he could see, but it produced an immediate effect. For again Scrooge saw himself. He was older now; a man in the prime of life. His face had not the harsh and rigid lines of later years; but it had begun to wear the signs of care and avarice. There was an eager, greedy, restless motion in the eye, which showed the passion that had taken root, and where the shadow of the growing tree would fall.

He was not alone, but sat by the side of a fair young girl in a mourning-dress: in whose eyes there were tears, which sparkled in the light that shone out of the Ghost of Christmas Past.

"It matters little," she said, softly. "To you, very little. Another idol has displaced me; and if it can cheer and comfort you in time to come, as I would have tried to do, I have no just cause to grieve."

"What Idol has displaced you?" he rejoined.

"A golden one."

"This is the even-handed dealing of the world!" he said. "There is nothing on which it is so hard as poverty; and there is nothing it professes to condemn with such severity as the pursuit of wealth!"

"You fear the world too much," she answered, gently.

"All your other hopes have merged into the hope of being beyond the chance of its sordid reproach. I have seen your nobler aspirations fall off one by one, until the master-passion, Gain, engrosses you. Have I not?"

"What then?" he retorted. "Even if I have grown so much wiser, what then? I am not changed towards you."

She shook her head.

"Am I?"

"Our contract is an old one. It was made when we were both poor and content to be so, until, in good season, we could improve our worldly fortune by our patient industry. You are changed. When it was made, you were another man."

"I was a boy," he said impatiently.

"Your own feeling tells you that you were not what you are," she returned. "I am. That which promised happiness when we were one in heart, is fraught with misery now that we are two. How often and how keenly I have thought of this, I will not say. It is enough that I have thought of it, and can release you."

"Have I ever sought release?"

"In words. No. Never."

"In what, then?"

"In a changed nature; in an altered spirit; in another atmosphere of life; another Hope as its great end. In everything that made my love of any worth or value in your sight. If this had never been between us," said the girl, looking mildly, but with steadiness, upon him; "tell me, would you seek me out and try to win me now? Ah, no!"

He seemed to yield to the justice of this supposition, in spite of himself. But he said with a struggle, "You think not."

"I would gladly think otherwise if I could," she answered, "Heaven knows! When I have learned a Truth like this, I know how strong and irresistible it must be. But if you were free to-day, to-morrow, yesterday, can even I believe that you would choose a dowerless girl—you who, in your very confidence with her, weigh everything by Gain: or, choosing her, if for a moment you were false enough to your one guiding principle to do so, do I not know that your repentance and regret would surely follow? I do; and I release you. With a full heart, for the love of him you once were."

He was about to speak; but with her head turned from him, she resumed.

"You may—the memory of what is past half makes me hope you will—have pain in this. A very, very brief time, and you will dismiss the recollection of it, gladly, as an unprofitable dream, from which it happened well that you awoke. May you be happy in the life you have chosen!"

She left him, and they parted.

"Spirit!" said Scrooge, "show me no more! Conduct me home. Why do you delight to torture me?"

"One shadow more!" exclaimed the Ghost.

"No more!" cried Scrooge. "No more. I don't wish to see it. Show me no more!"

But the relentless Ghost pinioned him in both his arms, and forced him to observe what happened next.

They were in another scene and place; a room, not very large or handsome, but full of comfort. Near to the winter fire sat a beautiful young girl, so like that last that Scrooge believed it was the same, until he saw her, now a comely matron, sitting opposite her daughter. The noise in this room was perfectly tumultuous, for there were more children there, than Scrooge in his agitated state of mind could count; and, unlike the celebrated herd in the poem, they were not forty children conducting themselves like one, but every child was conducting itself like forty. The consequences were uproarious beyond belief; but no one seemed to care; on the contrary, the mother and daughter laughed heartily, and enjoyed it very much; and the latter, soon beginning to mingle in the sports, got pillaged by the young brigands most ruthlessly. What would I not have given to be one of them! Though I never could have been so rude, no, no! I wouldn't for the wealth of all the world have crushed that braided hair, and torn it down; and for the precious little shoe, I wouldn't have plucked it off, God bless my soul! to save my life. As to measuring her waist in sport, as they did, bold young brood, I couldn't have done it; I should have expected my arm to have grown round it for a punishment, and never come straight again. And yet I should have dearly liked, I own, to have touched her lips; to have questioned her, that she might have opened them; to have looked upon the lashes of her downcast eyes, and never raised a blush; to have let loose waves of hair, an inch of which would be a keepsake beyond price: in short, I should have liked, I do confess, to have had the lightest licence of a child, and yet to have been man enough to know its value.

But now a knocking at the door was heard, and such a rush immediately ensued that she with laughing face and plundered dress was borne towards it the centre of a flushed and boisterous group, just in time to greet the father, who came home attended by a man laden with Christmas toys and presents. Then the shouting and the struggling, and the onslaught that was made on the defenceless porter! The scaling him with chairs for ladders to dive into his pockets, despoil him of brown-paper parcels, hold on tight by his cravat, hug him round his neck, pommel his back, and kick his legs in irrepressible affection! The shouts of wonder and delight with which the development of every package was received! The terrible announcement that the baby had been taken in the act of putting a doll's frying-pan into his mouth, and was more than suspected of having swallowed a fictitious turkey, glued on a wooden platter! The immense relief of finding this a false alarm! The joy, and gratitude, and ecstasy! They are all indescribable alike. It is enough that by degrees the children and their emotions got out of the parlour, and by one stair at a time, up to the top of the house; where they went to bed, and so subsided.

And now Scrooge looked on more attentively than ever, when the master of the house, having his daughter leaning fondly on him, sat down with her and her mother at his own fireside; and when he thought that such another creature, quite as graceful and as full of promise, might have called him father, and been a spring-time in the haggard winter of his life, his sight grew very dim indeed.

"Belle," said the husband, turning to his wife with a smile, "I saw an old friend of yours this afternoon."

"Who was it?"

"Guess!"

"How can I? Tut, don't I know?" she added in the same breath, laughing as he laughed. "Mr. Scrooge."

"Mr. Scrooge it was. I passed his office window; and as it was not shut up, and he had a candle inside, I could scarcely help seeing him. His partner, I do not know his name, had been killed in the violence in the city. I considered going inside but it was so dark and miserable and there he sat alone. Quite alone in the world, I do believe. Many of the buildings nearby are empty, I fear their occupants were killed by the creatures or, and I sincerely hope this, they may have simply abandoned them, perhaps in the hope of returning soon."

"Spirit!" said Scrooge in a broken voice, "remove me from this place."

"I told you these were shadows of the things that have been," said the Ghost. "That they are what they are, do not blame me!"

"Remove me!" Scrooge exclaimed, "I cannot bear it!"

The ground shook and darkened around the group before they were replaced by the dark wall of some building. Scrooge at first assumed he was back at home until he recognised Marley, exactly as he had been seven years ago.

"No, not this!" exclaimed Scrooge as he looked feverishly from left to right.

"Why do you recoil from the sight of your old partner? Are you not joyful to see him once again and in such good health?" asked the Spirit.

"Of course not!" answered Scrooge with barely concealed anger. "His death wasn't my fault, how could it be?" he cried.

"Yet you show regret and remorse over this place. Watch!" said the Spirit, as it stretched out its arms towards a slightly younger Scrooge and Marley in the Bank.

The two men were making their way out of the Bank when a great cry came from the street outside. As Scrooge and the Spirit moved out into the open, they could both clearly see the front of a massive crowd coming up the hill. In front of the crowd were small numbers of panicked citizens, some carrying children and others armfuls of possessions. Screams and shouts came from them as they rushed past the front of the Bank and disappeared off into the distant streets.

"Watch carefully, who are these people?" asked the Spirit, as it pointed to a group of about a dozen scruffy children and a handful of adults that ran inside the Bank.

As they watched, the younger Marley and Scrooge rushed inside after them. The Spirit beckoned to the horde coming up the hill and Scrooge watched in despair as they entered the square. The group were the filthy, blood dripping undead and they all made their way around the Bank. As the closest drew near, Scrooge lifted up his hands to protect himself yet they moved through him.

"This is what has past, this cannot be changed," said the Spirit.

As they watched, the crowd of undead surrounded the building as though it were some kind of sacred site. Their movement was as though they were a great wave or flood that engulfed a mountaintop so that it became an island. In moments the entire building was surrounded by a thick mass of them, so that no living soul could enter or leave the safety of the old building.

Once fully encircled, those closest to the Bank turned their attention to the windows and doors as they forced their way inside through any part of the building able to be damaged or torn open. A small number of firearms were discharged, presumably from guards or citizens, though the number of shots was pathetically small and had no effect on the great number crashing inside.

"Why did they do this?" asked a quivering Scrooge, "I never understood why they wanted to control that place of all things."

"Because there is something there that controls them," said the Spirit, pointing to the floor of the Bank.

"This building stands upon the ruins of something much older, darker and more evil than even you can fathom. It was built many centuries ago and has a power even I cannot fathom or hope to influence. Whoever controls the artefact and this evil place will be able to control the walking dead," continued the Spirit.

The two entered the Bank, watching the swirling melee as the monsters attacked and tore apart any living person they could reach. The violence was horrendous as the creatures used their hands, nails and even teeth in a battle that reminded Scrooge of some of the accounts of the End of Days. In the middle of the room stood Marley and the younger Scrooge, both holding their sticks and fighting like demented mad men as the creatures tried to get nearer to them.

"Impressive, I see your swordsmanship came in useful after all. Pity you never kept it up," said the Spirit wryly.

Scrooge watched for a moment, surprised at the skill he showed with such a simple weapon. He almost started to replicate the movements before he noticed a man dragged to the ground, his throat bitten into by an undead thing. As he stopped, he turned around to see the slightly younger Scrooge almost knocked to the ground but a cunningly concealed pocket pistol, with half a dozen tiny barrels, appeared from inside his coat and discharged a cloud of lead pellets that blasted back the two closest assailants. He followed up his shot with several strong strikes with the cane that cleared a few feet of space around him.

Somewhere outside came a multitude of cracking sounds that Scrooge instantly recognised as gunfire. Hints of white smoke washed inside from the volley of musketry followed by a dozen men in bright uniforms dashing inside. They were the local yeomanry, a mounted city militia and well capable of fighting the undead. From outside the sound of more gunfire heralded the arrival of more soldiers. As the fighting continued unseen outside, the group of sword and pistol-armed soldiers fought their way inside. Several of them were dragged to the ground by the creatures, while the remainder emptied their flintlock pistols into the horde whilst hacking and slashing away with their curved swords.

A strange group of foreign looking men in red cloth and carrying a metal case were trying to make their way discreetly to a side door. They had come from outside the Bank and looked like no men he had ever seen before or since in England. The undead ignored them as though they were one of their own, though they were unmistakably different in both clothing and movement, as well as the fact that they were alive. They had a look that reminded him of the tale he had heard of the Thuggee in India but he had never met one in person. One of the soldiers managed to make his way to them and was instantly attacked with a savage looking curved sword. The soldier succeeded in defending himself with his own sword, only to be attacked from behind by a small group of the undead. As they dragged him to the ground, the group in red continued towards the doors at the back of the Bank.

Scrooge covered his face as the scenes of horror around him filled him with dread.

"Who are they, I don't remember them?" asked Scrooge.

"Well, you were somewhat preoccupied," said the Spirit with a smile, as it pointed to Marley and Scrooge who were fighting their way out to the soldiers.

"They were trying to take the artefact below the Bank. If it were not for what happened next you would have suffered the same fate as those outside," said the Spirit.

Though the two men were hardly young soldiers they gave a surprisingly vigorous defence, each of them being responsible for toppling four or five of the creatures. The group of four men in red approached Marley and Scrooge, looking to move past them and into the bowels of the building. One struck Marley with his fist, knocking the old man to the ground whilst the others pushed past. Scrooge swung his cane and smashed the man in the temple, sending him to the ground making the other three lose control of whatever they seemed to be carrying. As the artefact fell, it struck the ground, chunks of old metal tumbling from its insides. A volley of musketry struck two of the men leaving just one wounded and another still fighting Scrooge. As the soldiers overpowered the undead and reached the centre of the room, they formed a defensive position around the artefact, keeping the remaining men in red away from it. By some miracle, none of the undead attacked those who were in close proximity of the artefact or its remains and the soldiers were able to carry it safely from the Bank and towards the doors whilst more soldiers rushed in. With the tide turning, Marley and Scrooge both made for the door, looking to get as far away from building as possible.

As Scrooge reached the safety of the door he could be seen turning back looking for Marley, who was wrestling with a man over a chest or crate of some kind. As Scrooge looked closer, it seemed the item was a strongbox, probably one looted from the Bank.

Scrooge shouted in vain to Marley who could hear nothing from his future self.

"Marley, stay with the artefact you fool!" he cried, as his memories of the event appeared fresh.

It was pointless though, and one of the zombies broke

from the crowd and struck Marley and as they tried to escape, the entire group disappeared in a swirling melee of ruffians, soldiers and the drooling walking dead, who now seemed interested in just attacking or killing anybody around them.

"Greed and selfish desires brought down Marley. He could have left with you but instead he stayed behind to safeguard more money, money that was not even his to guard. Your fate is still tied to him Mr. Scrooge, are you any different?" it said.

Scrooge turned away from the scene, clearly knowing what had happened to Marley. In his heart, he knew that he would have grabbed the strongbox as well had he noticed it before he reached the door. It was simple chance that had saved him on that day. His avarice could have brought him down as easily as Marley. This simple fact shook him hard.

"It could have been me," he muttered to himself, "me!"

He turned upon the Ghost, and seeing that it looked upon him with a face, in which in some strange way there were fragments of all the faces it had shown him, wrestled with it.

"Leave me! Take me back. Haunt me no longer!"

In the struggle, if that can be called a struggle in which the Ghost with no visible resistance on its own part was undisturbed by any effort of its adversary, Scrooge observed that its light was burning high and bright; and dimly connecting that with its influence over him, he seized the extinguisher-cap, and by a sudden action pressed it down upon its head.

The Spirit dropped beneath it, so that the extinguisher covered its whole form; but though Scrooge pressed it down with all his force, he could not hide the light: which streamed from under it, in an unbroken flood upon the ground.

He was conscious of being exhausted, and overcome by an irresistible drowsiness; and, further, of being in his own bedroom. He gave the cap a parting squeeze, in which his hand relaxed; and had barely time to reel to bed, before he sank into a heavy sleep.

A ZOMBIE CHRISTMAS CAROL

STAVE THREE

THE SECOND OF THE THREE SPIRITS.

Awaking in the middle of a prodigiously tough snore, and sitting up in bed to get his thoughts together, Scrooge had no occasion to be told that the bell was again upon the stroke of One. He felt that he was restored to consciousness in the right nick of time, for the especial purpose of holding a conference with the second messenger despatched to him through Jacob Marley's intervention. But finding that he turned uncomfortably cold when he began to wonder which of his curtains this new spectre would draw back, he put them every one aside with his own hands; and lying down again, established a sharp look-out all round the bed. For he wished to challenge the Spirit on the moment of its appearance, and did not wish to be taken by surprise, and made nervous.

Gentlemen of the free-and-easy sort, who plume themselves on being acquainted with a move or two, and being usually equal to the time-of-day, express the wide range of their capacity for adventure by observing that they are good for anything from pitch-and-toss to manslaughter; between which opposite extremes, no doubt, there lies a tolerably wide and comprehensive range of subjects. Without venturing for Scrooge quite as hardily as this, I don't mind calling on you to believe that he was ready for a good broad field of strange appearances, and that nothing between a baby and rhinoceros would have astonished him very much.

Now, being prepared for almost anything, he was not by any means prepared for nothing; and, consequently, when the Bell struck One, and no shape appeared, he was taken with a violent fit of trembling. Five minutes, ten minutes, a quarter of an hour went by, yet nothing came. All this time, he lay upon his bed, the very core and centre of a blaze of ruddy light, which streamed upon it when the clock proclaimed the hour; and which, being only light, was more alarming than a dozen ghosts, as he was powerless to make out what it meant, or would be at; and was sometimes apprehensive that he might be at that very moment an interesting case of spontaneous combustion, without having the consolation of knowing it. At last, however, he began to think—as you or I would have thought at first; for it is always the person not in the predicament who knows what ought to have been done in it, and would unquestionably have done it too—at last, I say, he began to think that the source and secret of this ghostly light might be in the adjoining room, from whence, on further tracing it, it seemed to shine. This idea taking full possession of his mind, he got up softly and shuffled in his slippers to the door.

The moment Scrooge's hand was on the lock, a strange voice called him by his name, and bade him enter. He obeyed.

It was his own room. There was no doubt about that. But it had undergone a surprising transformation. The walls and ceiling were so hung with living green, that it looked a perfect grove; from every part of which, bright gleaming berries glistened. The crisp leaves of holly, mistletoe, and ivy reflected back the light, as if so many little mirrors had been scattered there; and such a mighty blaze went roaring up the chimney, as that dull petrification of a hearth had never known in Scrooge's time, or Marley's, or for many and many a winter season gone.

Heaped up on the floor, to form a kind of throne, were turkeys, geese, game, poultry, brawn, great joints of meat, sucking-pigs, long wreaths of sausages, mince-pies, plum-puddings, barrels of oysters, red-hot chestnuts, cherry-cheeked apples, juicy oranges, luscious pears, immense twelfth-cakes, and seething bowls of punch, that made the chamber dim with their delicious steam. In easy state upon this couch, there sat a jolly Giant, glorious to see; who bore a glowing torch, in shape not unlike Plenty's horn, and held it up, high up, to shed its light on Scrooge, as he came peeping round the door.

"Come in!" exclaimed the Ghost. "Come in! and know me better, man!"

Scrooge entered timidly, and hung his head before this Spirit. He was not the dogged Scrooge he had been; and though the Spirit's eyes were clear and kind, he did not like to meet them.

"I am the Ghost of Christmas Present," said the Spirit. "Look upon me!"

Scrooge reverently did so. It was clothed in one simple green robe, or mantle, bordered with white fur. This garment hung so loosely on the figure, that its capacious breast was bare, as if disdaining to be warded or concealed by any artifice. Its feet, observable beneath the ample folds of the garment, were also bare; and on its head it wore no other covering than a holly wreath, set here and there with shining icicles. Its dark brown curls were long and free; free as its genial face, its sparkling eye, its open hand, its cheery voice, its unconstrained demeanour, and its joyful air. Girded round its middle was an antique scabbard; but no sword was in it, and the ancient sheath was eaten up with rust. It looked remarkably similar to the scabbard carried by the old soldier Mr. Jenkins but even older if that were possible. It certainly looked old and fitted around the Spirit in a fashion that implied it was comfortable and experienced in carrying it.

SCROOGE'S THIRD VISITOR

"You have never seen the like of me before!" exclaimed the Spirit.

"Never," Scrooge made answer to it.

"Have never walked forth with the younger members of my family; meaning (for I am very young) my elder brothers born in these later years?" pursued the Phantom.

"Are your brothers Spirits or are they like the creatures that killed old Marley? Those evil and insister spirits of the dead that rise and attack the living? Is that why you are here?" asked Scrooge.

A chill wind filled the room as the Ghost stared at Scrooge but refused to answer his question. It was obvious from its mood and the ill wind that he had asked a foul or inappropriate question.

"Then I don't think I have," said Scrooge. "I am afraid I have not. Have you had many brothers, Spirit?"

"More than eighteen hundred," said the Ghost.

"A tremendous family to provide for, you must be rich in money or friends!" muttered Scrooge.

The Ghost of Christmas Present rose.

"Spirit," said Scrooge submissively, "conduct me

where you will. I went forth last night on compulsion, and I learnt a lesson which is working now. To-night, if you have aught to teach me, let me profit by it."

"This night you will see the calamity that is befalling the people of this place. Are you ready to see and learn?" it asked.

Scrooge nodded in both agreement and fear.

"Touch my robe!"

Scrooge did as he was told, and held it fast.

Holly, mistletoe, red berries, ivy, turkeys, geese, game, poultry, brawn, meat, pigs, sausages, oysters, pies, puddings, fruit, and punch, all vanished instantly. So did the room, the fire, the ruddy glow, the hour of night, and they stood in the city streets on Christmas morning, where (for the weather was severe) the people made a rough, but brisk and not unpleasant kind of music, in scraping the snow from the pavement in front of their dwellings, and from the tops of their houses, whence it was mad delight to the boys to see it come plumping down into the road below, and splitting into artificial little snow-storms.

The house fronts looked black enough, and the windows blacker, contrasting with the smooth white sheet of snow upon the roofs, and with the dirtier snow upon the ground; which last deposit had been ploughed up in deep furrows by the heavy wheels of carts and waggons; furrows that crossed and re-crossed each other hundreds of times where the great streets branched off;

and made intricate channels, hard to trace in the thick yellow mud and icy water. The sky was gloomy, and the shortest streets were choked up with a dingy mist, half thawed, half frozen, whose heavier particles descended in a shower of sooty atoms, as if all the chimneys in Great Britain had, by one consent, caught fire, and were blazing away to their dear hearts' content. There was nothing very cheerful in the climate or the town, and yet was there an air of cheerfulness abroad that the clearest summer air and brightest summer sun might have endeavoured to diffuse in vain.

For, the people who were shovelling away on the housetops were jovial and full of glee; calling out to one another from the parapets, and now and then exchanging a facetious snowball—better-natured missile far than many a wordy jest—laughing heartily if it went right and not less heartily if it went wrong. The poulterers' shops were still half open, and the fruiterers' were radiant in their glory. There were great, round, pot-bellied baskets of chestnuts, shaped like the waistcoats of jolly old gentlemen, lolling at the doors, and tumbling out into the street in their apoplectic opulence. There were ruddy, brown-faced, broad-girthed Spanish Onions, shining in the fatness of their growth like Spanish Friars, and winking from their shelves in wanton slyness at the girls as they went by, and glanced demurely at the hung-up mistletoe. There were pears and apples, clustered high in blooming pyramids;

there were bunches of grapes, made, in the shopKeepers' benevolence to dangle from conspicuous hooks, that people's mouths might water gratis as they passed; there were piles of filberts, mossy and brown, recalling, in their fragrance, ancient walks among the woods, and pleasant shufflings ankle deep through withered leaves; there were Norfolk Biffins, squat and swarthy, setting off the yellow of the oranges and lemons, and, in the great compactness of their juicy persons, urgently entreating and beseeching to be carried home in paper bags and eaten after dinner. The very gold and silver fish, set forth among these choice fruits in a bowl, though members of a dull and stagnant-blooded race, appeared to know that there was something going on; and, to a fish, went gasping round and round their little world in slow and passionless excitement.

The Grocers'! oh, the Grocers'! nearly closed, with perhaps two shutters down, or one; but through those gaps such glimpses! It was not alone that the scales descending on the counter made a merry sound, or that the twine and roller parted company so briskly, or that the canisters were rattled up and down like juggling tricks, or even that the blended scents of tea and coffee were so grateful to the nose, or even that the raisins were so plentiful and rare, the almonds so extremely white, the sticks of cinnamon so long and straight, the other spices so delicious, the candied fruits so caked and spotted with molten sugar as to make the coldest lookers-on feel faint and subsequently bilious. Nor was it that the figs were moist and pulpy, or that the French plums blushed in modest tartness from their highly-decorated boxes, or that everything was good to eat and in its Christmas dress; but the customers were all so hurried and so eager in the hopeful promise of the day, that they tumbled up against each other at the door, crashing their wicker baskets wildly, and left their purchases upon the counter, and came running back to fetch them, and committed hundreds of the like mistakes, in the best humour possible; while the Grocer and his people were so frank and fresh that the polished hearts with which they fastened their aprons behind might have been their own, worn outside for general inspection, and for Christmas daws to peck at if they chose.

But soon the steeples called good people all, to church and chapel, and away they came, flocking through the streets in their best clothes, and with their gayest faces. And at the same time there emerged from scores of bye-streets, lanes, and nameless turnings, innumerable people, carrying their dinners to the bakers' shops. The sight of these poor revellers appeared to interest the Spirit very much, for he stood with Scrooge beside him in a baker's doorway, and taking off the covers as their bearers passed, sprinkled incense on their dinners from his torch. And it was a very uncommon kind of torch, for once or twice when there were angry words between some dinner-carriers who had jostled each other, he shed a few drops of water on them from it, and their good humour was restored directly. For they said, it was a shame to quarrel upon Christmas Day. And so it was! God love it, so it was!

In time the bells ceased, and the bakers were shut up; and yet there was a genial shadowing forth of all these dinners and the progress of their cooking, in the thawed blotch of wet above each baker's oven; where the pavement smoked as if its stones were cooking too.

"Is there a peculiar flavour in what you sprinkle from your torch?" asked Scrooge.

"There is. My own."

"Would it apply to any kind of dinner on this day?" asked Scrooge.

"To any kindly given. To a poor one most."

"Why to a poor one most?" asked Scrooge.

"Because it needs it most."

"Spirit," said Scrooge, after a moment's thought, "I wonder you, of all the beings in the many worlds about us, should desire to cramp these people's opportunities of innocent enjoyment."

"I!" cried the Spirit.

"You would deprive them of their means of dining every seventh day, often the only day on which they can be said to dine at all," said Scrooge. "Wouldn't you?"

"I!" cried the Spirit.

"You seek to close these places on the Seventh Day?" said Scrooge. "And it comes to the same thing."

"I seek!" exclaimed the Spirit.

"Forgive me if I am wrong. It has been done in your name, or at least in that of your family," said Scrooge.

"There are some upon this earth of yours," returned the Spirit, "who lay claim to know us, and who do their deeds of passion, pride, ill-will, hatred, envy, bigotry, and selfishness in our name, who are as strange to us and all our kith and kin, as if they had never lived. Remember that, and charge their doings on themselves, not us."

Scrooge promised that he would; and they went on, invisible, as they had been before, into the suburbs of the town. It was a remarkable quality of the Ghost (which Scrooge had observed at the baker's), that notwithstanding his gigantic size, he could accommodate himself to any place with ease; and that he stood beneath a low roof quite as gracefully and like a supernatural creature, as it was possible he could have done in any lofty hall.

And perhaps it was the pleasure the good Spirit had in showing off this power of his, or else it was his own kind, generous, hearty nature, and his sympathy with all poor men, that led him straight to Scrooge's clerk's; for there he went, and took Scrooge with him, holding to his robe; and on the threshold of the door the Spirit smiled, and stopped to bless Bob Cratchit's dwelling with the sprinkling of his torch. Think of that! Bob had but fifteen "Bob" a-week himself; he pocketed on Saturdays but fifteen copies of his Christian name; and yet the Ghost of Christmas Present blessed his four-roomed house!

Then up rose Mrs. Cratchit, Cratchit's wife, dressed out but poorly in a twice-turned gown, but brave in ribbons, which are cheap and make a goodly show for sixpence; and she laid the cloth, assisted by Belinda Cratchit, second of her daughters, also brave in ribbons; while Master Peter Cratchit plunged a fork into the saucepan of potatoes, and getting the corners of his monstrous shirt collar (Bob's private property, conferred upon his son and heir in honour of the day) into his mouth, rejoiced to find himself so gallantly attired, and yearned to show his linen in the fashionable Parks. And now two smaller Cratchits, boy and girl, came tearing in, screaming that outside the baker's they had smelt the goose, and known it for their own; and basking in luxurious thoughts of sage and onion, these young Cratchits danced about the table, and exalted Master Peter Cratchit to the skies, while he (not proud, although his collars nearly choked him) blew the fire, until the slow potatoes bubbling up, knocked loudly at the saucepan-lid to be let out and peeled.

"What has ever got your precious father then?" said Mrs. Cratchit. "And your brother, Tiny Tim! And Martha warn't as late last Christmas Day by half-an-hour?"

"Here's Martha, mother!" said a girl, appearing as she spoke.

"Here's Martha, mother!" cried the two young Cratchits. "Hurrah! There's such a goose, Martha!"

"Why, bless your heart alive, my dear, how late you are!" said Mrs. Cratchit, kissing her a dozen times, and taking off her shawl and bonnet for her with officious zeal.

"We'd a deal of work to finish up last night," replied the girl, "and had to clear away this morning, mother!"

"Well! Never mind so long as you are come," said Mrs. Cratchit. "Sit ye down before the fire, my dear, and have a warm, Lord bless ye!"

"No, no! There's father coming," cried the two young Cratchits, who were everywhere at once. "Hide, Martha, hide!"

So Martha hid herself, and in came little Bob, the father, with at least three feet of comforter exclusive of the fringe, hanging down before him; and his threadbare clothes darned up and brushed, to look seasonable; and Tiny Tim upon his shoulder. Alas for Tiny Tim, he bore a little crutch, and had his limbs supported by an iron frame!

"Why, where's our Martha?" cried Bob Cratchit, looking round.

"Not coming," said Mrs. Cratchit.

"Not coming!" said Bob, with a sudden declension in his high spirits; for he had been Tim's blood horse all the way from church, and had come home rampant. "Not coming upon Christmas Day!"

Martha didn't like to see him disappointed, if it were only in joke; so she came out prematurely from behind the closet door, and ran into his arms, while the two young Cratchits hustled Tiny Tim, and bore him off into the wash-house, that he might hear the pudding singing in the copper.

"And how did little Tim behave?" asked Mrs. Cratchit, when she had rallied Bob on his credulity, and Bob had hugged his daughter to his heart's content.

"As good as gold," said Bob, "and better. Somehow he gets thoughtful, sitting by himself so much, and thinks the strangest things you ever heard. He told me, coming home, that he hoped the people saw him in the church, because he was a cripple, and it might be pleasant to them to remember upon Christmas Day, who made lame beggars walk, and blind men see."

Bob's voice was tremulous when he told them this, and trembled more when he said that Tiny Tim was growing strong and hearty.

His active little crutch was heard upon the floor, and back came Tiny Tim before another word was spoken, escorted by his brother and sister to his stool before the fire; and while Bob, turning up his cuffs—as if, poor fellow, they were capable of being made more shabby— compounded some hot mixture in a jug with gin and lemons, and stirred it round and round and put it on the hob to simmer; Master Peter, and the two ubiquitous young Cratchits went to fetch the goose, with which they soon returned in high procession.

Such a bustle ensued that you might have thought a goose the rarest of all birds; a feathered phenomenon, to which a black swan was a matter of course—and in truth it was something very like it in that house. Mrs. Cratchit made the gravy (ready beforehand in a little saucepan) hissing hot; Master Peter mashed the potatoes with incredible vigour; Miss Belinda sweetened up the apple-sauce; Martha dusted the hot plates; Bob took Tiny Tim beside him in a tiny corner at the table; the two young Cratchits set chairs for everybody, not forgetting themselves, and mounting guard upon their posts, crammed spoons into their mouths, lest they should shriek for goose before their turn came to be helped. At last the dishes were set on, and grace was said. It was succeeded by a breathless pause, as Mrs. Cratchit, looking slowly all along the carving-knife, prepared to plunge it in the breast; but when she did, and when the long expected gush of stuffing issued forth, one murmur of delight arose all round the board, and even Tiny Tim, excited by the two young Cratchits, beat on the table with the handle of his knife, and feebly cried Hurrah!

There never was such a goose. Bob said he didn't believe there ever was such a goose cooked. Its tenderness and flavour, size and cheapness, were the themes of universal admiration. Eked out by apple-sauce and mashed potatoes, it was a sufficient dinner for the whole family; indeed, as Mrs. Cratchit said with great delight (surveying one small atom of a bone upon the dish), they hadn't ate it all at last! Yet every one had had enough, and the youngest Cratchits in particular, were steeped in sage and onion to the eyebrows! But now, the plates being changed by Miss Belinda, Mrs. Cratchit left the room alone—too nervous to bear witnesses—to take the pudding up and bring it in.

Suppose it should not be done enough! Suppose it should break in turning out! Suppose somebody should have got over the wall of the back-yard, and stolen it, while they were merry with the goose—a supposition at which the two young Cratchits became livid! All sorts of horrors were supposed.

Hallo! A great deal of steam! The pudding was out of the copper. A smell like a washing-day! That was the cloth. A smell like an eating-house and a pastrycook's next door to each other, with a laundress's next door to that! That was the pudding! In half a minute Mrs. Cratchit entered—flushed, but smiling proudly—with the pudding, like a speckled cannon-ball, so hard and firm, blazing in half of half-a-quartern of ignited brandy, and bedight with Christmas holly stuck into the top.

Oh, a wonderful pudding! Bob Cratchit said, and calmly too, that he regarded it as the greatest success achieved by Mrs. Cratchit since their marriage. Mrs. Cratchit said that now the weight was off her mind, she would confess she had had her doubts about the quantity of flour. Everybody had something to say about it, but nobody said or thought it was at all a small pudding for a large family. It would have been flat heresy to do so. Any Cratchit would have blushed to hint at such a thing.

At last the dinner was all done, the cloth was cleared, the hearth swept, and the fire made up. The compound in the jug being tasted, and considered perfect, apples and oranges were put upon the table, and a shovel-full of chestnuts on the fire. Then all the Cratchit family drew round the hearth, in what Bob Cratchit called a circle, meaning half a one; and at Bob Cratchit's elbow stood the family display of glass. Two tumblers, and a custard-cup without a handle.

These held the hot stuff from the jug, however, as well as golden goblets would have done; and Bob served it out with beaming looks, while the chestnuts on the fire sputtered and cracked noisily. Then Bob proposed:

"A Merry Christmas to us all, my dears. God bless us!"

Which all the family re-echoed.

"God bless us every one!" said Tiny Tim, the last of all.

He sat very close to his father's side upon his little stool. Bob held his withered little hand in his, as if he loved the child, and wished to keep him by his side, and dreaded that he might be taken from him.

"Spirit," said Scrooge, with an interest he had never felt before, "tell me if Tiny Tim will live."

"I see a vacant seat," replied the Ghost, "in the poor chimney-corner, and a crutch without an owner. If these shadows remain unaltered by the Future, the child will die as will all the family here."

"No, no," said Scrooge. "Oh, no, kind Spirit! say they will be spared."

"If these shadows remain unaltered by the Future, none other of my race," returned the Ghost, "will find them here. What then? If he and the rest are like to die, they had better do it, and decrease the surplus population."

Scrooge hung his head to hear his own words quoted by the Spirit, and was overcome with penitence and grief.

"Tell me Spirit, why will they die? I see that Tiny Tim is frail and vulnerable, but the rest of his family appear strong and they care for themselves as well as they ought."

"Man," said the Ghost, "if man you be in heart, not adamant, forbear that wicked cant until you have discovered What the surplus is, and Where it is. Will you decide what men shall live, what men shall die? It may be, that in the sight of Heaven, you are more worthless and less fit to live than millions like this poor man's child. Oh God! to hear the Insect on the leaf pronouncing on the too much life among his hungry brothers in the dust!"

Scrooge bent before the Ghost's rebuke, and trembling cast his eyes upon the ground. But he raised them speedily, on hearing his own name.

"Mr. Scrooge!" said Bob; "I'll give you Mr. Scrooge, the Founder of the Feast!"

"The Founder of the Feast indeed!" cried Mrs. Cratchit, reddening. "I wish I had him here. I'd give him a piece of my mind to feast upon, and I hope he'd have a good appetite for it."

"My dear," said Bob, "the children! Christmas Day."

"It should be Christmas Day, I am sure," said she, "on which one drinks the health of such an odious, stingy, hard, unfeeling man as Mr. Scrooge. You know he is, Robert! Nobody knows it better than you do, poor fellow!"

"My dear," was Bob's mild answer, "Christmas Day."

"I'll drink his health for your sake and the Day's," said Mrs. Cratchit, "not for his. Long life to him! A merry Christmas and a happy new year! He'll be very merry and very happy, I have no doubt!"

The children drank the toast after her. It was the first of their proceedings which had no heartiness. Tiny Tim drank it last of all, but he didn't care twopence for it. Scrooge was the Ogre of the family. The mention of his name cast a dark shadow on the party, which was not dispelled for full five minutes.

After it had passed away, they were ten times merrier than before, from the mere relief of Scrooge the Baleful being done with. Bob Cratchit told them how he had a situation in his eye for Master Peter, which would bring in, if obtained, full five-and-sixpence weekly. The two young Cratchits laughed tremendously at the idea of Peter's being a man of business; and Peter himself looked thoughtfully at the fire from between his collars, as if he were deliberating what particular investments he should favour when he came into the receipt of that bewildering income. Martha, who was a poor apprentice at a milliner's, then told them what kind of work she had to do, and how many hours she worked at a stretch, and how she meant to lie abed to-morrow morning for a good long rest; to-morrow being a holiday she passed at home. Also how she had seen a countess and a lord some days before, and how the lord "was much about as tall as Peter;" at which Peter pulled up his collars so high that you couldn't have seen his head if you had been there. All this time the chestnuts and the jug went round and round; and by-and-bye they had a song, about a lost child travelling in the snow, from Tiny Tim, who had a plaintive little voice, and sang it very well indeed.

There was nothing of high mark in this. They were not a handsome family; they were not well dressed; their shoes were far from being water-proof; their clothes were scanty; and Peter might have known, and very likely did, the inside of a pawnbroker's. But, they were happy, grateful, pleased with one another, and contented with the time; and when they faded, and looked happier yet in the bright sprinklings of the Spirit's torch at parting, Scrooge had his eye upon them, and especially on Tiny Tim, until the last.

A loud clattering came from outside, quickly by a loud

banging on the door. Bob Cratchit looked in the direction and then back at his family. Miss Belinda made to move but he gestured for her to stay. He stood up and made his way to the door though he paused for a moment to check for anything suspicious. As he waited, a desperate banging came from a house further down the road. Mr Cratchit pushed open the door and stepped outside.

"Mr Cratchit, something evil approaches, it is attacking every house, run!" cried a boy as he rushed past.

"Evil?" he asked as he looked carefully down the street.

He concentrated watching for movement. Then he spotted the vanguard of the horde as it made its slow, methodical progress through the city. A series of screams came from a house just a few streets away. He was about to turn away when he spotted a young woman being chased. A person in ragged clothing grabbed her and knocked her to the ground. Mr Cratchit had seen enough and turned inside the house.

"Miss Belinda, the poker from the fire, quickly my child, have a care not to burn yourself!" he cried.

The child was quick and in moments handed the still hot poker, wrapped in a wet cloth at one end to him.

"Thank you, now lock the door behind me and do not open it unless you hear my voice, understood?" he said.

The young girl nodded and stepped back, pushing the door behind her. With a satisfying clunk, he heard the bolt as it slid carefully into place. He turned and checked on the state of the young woman, she was still on the ground and fighting for her life.

Rushing forward Scrooge reached the group and without hesitation, he struck the first in the chest. The blow was mighty and it sent the person stumbling backwards. As Mr Cratchit stepped forward to help the girl the man staggered forwards, him arms out in front, trying to grab him. With a deft movement he stepped to the man's side and swung the poker into the man's arm, it broke almost instantly with a sickening crunch.

"Leave us!" shouted Mr Cratchit.

It then simply turned towards him and that is when he finally saw the terrible face. It was the body of a man but the face of a corpse. The skin was pale white and the arms were scarred, and damaged.

"Lord save us!" cried Mr Cratchit as he stabbed the poker into the creature's chest.

As it howled, Mr Cratchit bent down and grabbed the young woman, helped her up and then rushed back to his home.

"Thank you, mister," said the woman as she tried to keep running.

As they reached the door, they both turned and looked back. The man was standing in the middle of the road with another dozen vile people not far behind. They watched in astonishment as he looked down at the metal spike in his chest and then looked back at Mr Cratchit. With a pathetic groaning, the thing started to stagger as though it was a corpse being dragged towards them.

Mr Cratchit knocked on the door in a particular sequence and called out, instantly it flew open to reveal his wife and children, all armed and waiting for danger.

"Inside!" ordered Mr Cratchit.

The two rushed through the door and as they entered the room Mrs Cratchit stepped forward and barred it shut.

"What's happening out there, Father?" asked Miss Belinda.

"I do not know, there is a group of evil men in the street, they were attacking this kind lady," he explained.

Martha looked at the woman, her face already pale.

"She does not look well, does she?" asked Tiny Tim.

"No she doesn't, help her to the table. Belinda, clear some space so we can lie her down. I will check her for wounds," said Mrs Cratchit.

With great effort, the little group moved the poorly woman to the table and lay her down carefully. As they looked at her, the front door started to shake.

"Children, watch the windows, I will guard the door," explained Bob Cratchit.

As they rushed into their positions one of the windows shattered and two scruffy men started to pull themselves inside. Miss Belinda rushed forward, bravely striking the first man with a pan. Tiny Tim joined in but their attacks seemed to do little to the foul figure. The first man already had one leg inside when Mr Cratchit arrived. In his hand he carried the carving knife and with precision that surprised them all forced in directly through the man's forehead.

"Oh, Lord!" cried Martha Cratchit as she covered her eyes.

The children recoiled at the violence but Bob, spurred on by his desire to protect his family, continued his attacks and managed to push them both out of the house.

"Tiny Tim, get some hammers and nails, we need to block the windows!" shouted Mr Cratchit.

The Spirit started to draw away from the home and with him Scrooge.

"Wait, we can't leave them like this!" said Scrooge.

The Spirit said nothing and in seconds, they had left the home and returned to the street. As they reached a distance from the evil scene, the unearthly creature pointed out into the distance. Scrooge strained his eyes but could see well enough to spot whatever calamity he had found.

"They grow closer and each step brings that family closer to death," he said with a chill that made Scrooge shudder.

By this time it was getting dark, and snowing pretty heavily; and as Scrooge and the Spirit went along the streets, there was no sign that anything untoward was happening or that any foul calamity would befall the inhabitants of the city. The brightness of the roaring fires in kitchens, parlours, and all sorts of rooms, was wonderful. Here, the flickering of the blaze showed preparations for a cosy dinner, with hot plates baking through and through before the fire, and deep red curtains, ready to be drawn to shut out cold and darkness. There all the children of the house were running out into the snow to meet their married sisters, brothers, cousins, uncles, aunts, and be the first to greet them. Here, again, were shadows on the window-blind of guests assembling; and there a group of handsome girls, all hooded and fur-booted, and all chattering at once, tripped lightly off to some near neighbour's house; where, woe upon the single man who saw them enter—artful witches, well they knew it—in a glow!

"What of the darkness though, these people will soon be under the grip of this evil tide!" cried Scrooge.

"Indeed, this is the price many will pay on this night if there is nobody that cares strongly enough to do something about it," said the Spirit.

The happiness and joy found by Scrooge helped to calm his mind and in just minutes he had forgotten about the darkness spoken of by the Spirit and was already enjoying the festivities and joy around him.

But, if you had judged from the numbers of people on their way to friendly gatherings, you might have thought that no one was at home to give them welcome when they got there, instead of every house expecting company, and piling up its fires half-chimney high. Blessings on it, how the Ghost exulted! How it bared its breadth of breast, and opened its capacious palm, and floated on, outpouring, with a generous hand, its bright and harmless mirth on everything within its reach! The very lamplighter, who ran on before, dotting the dusky street with specks of light, and who was dressed to spend the evening somewhere, laughed out loudly as the Spirit passed, though little kenned the lamplighter that he had any company but Christmas!

And now, without a word of warning from the Ghost, they stood upon a bleak and desert moor, where monstrous masses of rude stone were cast about, as though it were the burial-place of giants; and water spread itself wheresoever it listed, or would have done so, but for the frost that held it prisoner; and nothing grew but moss and furze, and coarse rank grass. Down in the west the setting sun had left a streak of fiery red, which glared upon the desolation for an instant, like a sullen eye, and frowning lower, lower, lower yet, was lost in the thick gloom of darkest night.

"What place is this?" asked Scrooge.

"A place where Miners live, who labour in the bowels of the earth," returned the Spirit. "But they know me. See!"

A light shone from the window of a hut, and swiftly they advanced towards it. Passing through the wall of mud and stone, they found a cheerful company assembled round a glowing fire. An old, old man and woman, with their children and their children's children, and another generation beyond that, all decked out gaily in their holiday attire. The old man, in a voice that seldom rose above the howling of the wind upon the barren waste, was singing them a Christmas song—it had been a very old song when he was a boy—and from time to time they all joined in the chorus. So surely as they raised their voices, the old man got quite blithe and loud; and so surely as they stopped, his vigour sank again.

The Spirit did not tarry here, but bade Scrooge hold his robe, and passing on above the moor, sped—whither? Not to sea? To sea. To Scrooge's horror, looking back, he saw the last of the land, a frightful range of rocks, behind them; and his ears were deafened by the thundering of water, as it rolled and roared, and raged among the dreadful caverns it had worn, and fiercely tried to undermine the earth.

Built upon a dismal reef of sunken rocks, some league or so from shore, on which the waters chafed and dashed, the wild year through, there stood a solitary lighthouse. Great heaps of sea-weed clung to its base, and storm-birds—born of the wind one might suppose, as sea-weed of the water—rose and fell about it, like the waves they skimmed.

But even here, two men who watched the light had made a fire, that through the loophole in the thick stone wall shed out a ray of brightness on the awful sea. Joining their horny hands over the rough table at which they sat, they wished each other Merry Christmas in their can of grog; and one of them: the elder, too, with his face all damaged and scarred with hard weather, as the figure-head of an old ship might be: struck up a sturdy song that was like a Gale in itself.

The sky darkened and all around Scrooge faded into a thick mist. As it cleared, he found himself behind a large stack of crates and boxes. The Spirit was nearby and looking out into a sizeable hall of some kind. Scrooge moved towards the Spirit and went to speak before the creature lifted its hand and placed a finger across its mouth, beckoning Scrooge to be silent.

"Where are we?" whispered Scrooge.

"We in the vaults of the National Provincial Bank, surely you recognise the place?" asked the Spirit.

The area was certainly not as one would expect to find in a Bank. It actually looked like a type of religious building that the Bank must have built over at some point in the past. Scrooge moved around the boxes and spotted a group of men, at least a dozen of them chanting in some form of ritual. They were kneeling in a circle around a golden object about the size of a wooden bucket. The item sat upon what appeared as a stone altar and carved into the ground itself.

"What are they doing?" asked Scrooge.

The Spirit drifted towards the group and Scrooge followed a short distance behind. As they approached the men, he was pleased to notice they could not see him. As his fear subsided, he moved closer, examining the people and the artefact in detail.

"How unusual. It is foreign, where is it from?" he asked.

"Overseas," came the cryptic and not particularly helpful reply.

Scrooge looked carefully. The object was a golden box, encrusted with jewels and detailed with inscriptions in a foreign looking tongue. The corners seemed gilded and it sat upon a red velvet pad. Scrooge was so busy watching that he did not notice the two men, each carrying a savage looking cudgel and dragging a scruffy looking child between them. As they came closer, Scrooge heard the noise and stepped aside, partially out of automatic courtesy and also to avoid being bumped into.

"Stop this instant!" he shouted but they ignored him and continued dragging the boy up until he was just feet away from the box. The two ruffians tied the young boy to the nearest column and in one swift motion tore part of his clothing away to reveal his arms.

Scrooge turned to the Spirit, pleading with it to do something but it simply stood silently, watching both the ceremony and Scrooge's reaction.

"Christmas is not all happy and joyous, as this homeless child is about to find," it said.

Scrooge turned back to see the two men carrying the velvet pad over to the boy. Another man who wore thick leather gloves much like those used for single stick fencing, opened the box, its hinges creaking with age to reveal a round, dull metal object. It looked damaged though from age or struggle who knew. The man lifted a fragment from the box and moved it close to the boy. As it approached his arm, his skin began to lighten and age. The man pulled it back and the aged skin stayed the same.

"What kind of evil madness is this?" cried Scrooge as he watched helplessly.

The boy struggled and shook as he tried unsuccessfully to escape as the man turned and shouted out to the rest of the assembled something in an evil, barbarian sounding tongue. The group of men all stood up, shouting in unison. As they cried out, they withdrew evil looking blades, much like the Indian tulwar blades he had seen in the past. They held the blades aloft as they continued their excited shouts.

Whilst this commotion continued, the boy had miraculously undone the rope on one hand and was feverishly pulling at the other. Scrooge moved up to the boy and encouraged him along, not that the boy could either see or hear the man.

"Come on, boy, the other arm o'er they will be on you in a flash. Come on!" he shouted in a mixture of fear and excitement.

The boy finally pulled the last bit of rope off, just in time to be observed by one of the two closest thugs. The man shouted as he pulled out his own curved sword and rushed to the boy. Not pausing for a moment the lad ducked past the first swing of the sword and rushed to the stairs. Scrooge chased after him, trying to encourage his escape. As the boy reached the top of the stairs, he pushed the door shut and vanished into the darkness above. Scrooge stopped, catching his breath before turning back to the Spirit. Before he was able to speak the group of armed men forced the door ajar and vanished in the same direction of the boy.

"Will he live?" asked a desperate Scrooge.

"For now. Unless something changes though, he will be dead this time Christmas Day."

"Dead? By their hands?" asked Scrooge.

"Dead by that artefact. It has the power of death."

"How do you know this to be true?" pleaded Scrooge.

Scrooge looked back into the room in the direction of where the artefact had sat. He walked over, looking at the marking on the ground. A howl like a strong wind came from the direction of the creature and Scrooge quickly looked up at its face.

"I know because it has happened before. You have already been shown what happened with Marley," said the Spirit.

"But why here? Cannot this artefact do harm elsewhere?" he asked.

"The artefact is remnant of a great evil from overseas. When brought to this place it gives the power of death and the ability to control the dead to whomever touches it."

"Is that what happened to Marley?"

The Spirit looked at Scrooge, but he could not tell from its expression whether it related to his death or not.

"Wait, I remember Marley fighting with somebody over an item. Was it the artefact?" asked Scrooge.

The Spirit turned his head.

"No, my dear Scrooge, he could have died to keep it safe, instead he was too busy with claiming more money," he said before turning back to the artefact.

"Where has it been all these years?" asked Scrooge.

"Nobody knows, it has been hidden away until this day," he said, before the room plunged into darkness.

Again the Ghost sped on, above the black and heaving sea—on, on—until, being far away, as he told Scrooge, from any shore, they lighted on a ship. They stood beside the helmsman at the wheel, the look-out in the bow, the officers who had the watch; dark, ghostly figures in their several stations; but every man among them hummed a Christmas tune, or had a Christmas thought, or spoke below his breath to his companion of some bygone Christmas Day, with homeward hopes belonging to it. And every man on board, waking or sleeping, good or bad, had had a kinder word for another on that day than on any day in the year; and had shared to some extent in its festivities; and had remembered those he cared for at a distance, and had known that they delighted to remember him.

He was shaken back to reality though as the Spirit took him below and into the bowels of the ship. It was dark and damp and just four small lamps lit the way. As they moved deep inside they came to a locked door. The Spirit waved his hand and Scrooge found himself inside the darkened room. He shuddered at the cold and glanced around, looking for something to hold onto. In the middle was a dark object yet a small glimmer of light from the planks above let in a little moonlight. It was a strong wooden crate of some kind. He moved forward to examine it only to find it missing a lid. As he looked inside, he found a few shards of metal but nothing of note. On the ground nearby was the body of a man, he was young, probably early twenties yet his body was contorted and pale as though he had been dead many weeks. Scrooge knelt down to examine him.

"What is wrong with him?"

"He has been gone for sometime but the object is already in London."

"What is it and why are they taking the container away?"

The Spirit looked at him but said nothing. Scrooge turned back moving his hand inside and reached out to touch the metal fragments.

"Do not touch them!" wailed the Spirit.

Scrooge fell back, terrified by the booming wail of the creature.

"This object is not earthly and is the cause of the scourge coming to your city. We must go."

Scrooge turned his head, hearing a noise coming from the dead man.

"Did you just hear something?" he asked of the Spirit.

The Spirit again ignored him and simply watched impassively as Scrooge approached the body and tried to find the source of the sound. It was all in vain though as the body answered the question by moving of its own accord.

Scrooge stumbled backwards, falling onto his back and making him yell out in pain. After a short pause, he lifted himself up into a sitting position only to find the dead man dragging himself over to Scrooge. As he came closer to him, he could see the decayed face and snapping jaws of some terrifying deranged beast. It was close enough to attack and it pushed forwards, shrieking in some ethereal and fearsome manner. Scrooge covered his face and screamed into the night.

It was a great surprise to Scrooge, while waiting for death to take him, and thinking what a solemn thing it was to move on through the lonely darkness over an unknown abyss, whose depths were secrets as profound as Death: it was a great surprise to Scrooge, while thus engaged, to hear a hearty laugh. It was a much greater surprise to Scrooge to recognise it as his own nephew's and to find himself in a bright, dry, gleaming room, with the Spirit standing smiling by his side, and looking at that same nephew with approving affability!

"Ha, ha!" laughed Scrooge's nephew. "Ha, ha, ha!"

Scrooge could barely contain himself and cried out in terror and joy at being away from the haunted vessel. It was a stark contrast between the fear of Scrooge and the joy of his nephew.

If you should happen, by any unlikely chance, to know a man more blest in a laugh than Scrooge's nephew, all I can say is, I should like to know him too. Introduce him to me, and I'll cultivate his acquaintance.

It is a fair, even-handed, noble adjustment of things, that while there is infection in disease and sorrow, there is nothing in the world so irresistibly contagious as laughter and good-humour. When Scrooge's nephew laughed in this way: holding his sides, rolling his head, and twisting his face into the most extravagant contortions: Scrooge's niece, by marriage, laughed as heartily as he. And their assembled friends being not a bit behindhand, roared out lustily.

"Ha, ha! Ha, ha, ha, ha!"

"He said that Christmas was a humbug, as I live!" cried Scrooge's nephew. "He believed it too!"

"More shame for him, Fred!" said Scrooge's niece, indignantly. Bless those women; they never do anything by halves. They are always in earnest.

She was very pretty: exceedingly pretty. With a dimpled, surprised-looking, capital face; a ripe little mouth, that seemed made to be kissed—as no doubt it was; all kinds of good little dots about her chin, that melted into one another when she laughed; and the sunniest pair of eyes you ever saw in any little creature's head. Altogether she was what you would have called provoking, you know; but satisfactory, too. Oh, perfectly satisfactory.

"He's a comical old fellow," said Scrooge's nephew, "that's the truth: and not so pleasant as he might be. However, his offences carry their own punishment, and I have nothing to say against him."

"I'm sure he is very rich, Fred," hinted Scrooge's niece. "At least you always tell me so."

"What of that, my dear!" said Scrooge's nephew. "His wealth is of no use to him. He don't do any good with it. He don't make himself comfortable with it. He hasn't the satisfaction of thinking—ha, ha, ha!—that he is ever going to benefit US with it."

"I have no patience with him," observed Scrooge's niece. Scrooge's niece's sisters, and all the other ladies, expressed the same opinion.

"Oh, I have!" said Scrooge's nephew. "I am sorry for him; I couldn't be angry with him if I tried. Who suffers by his ill whims! Himself, always. Here, he takes it into his head to dislike us, and he won't come and dine with us.

What's the consequence? He don't lose much of a dinner."

"Indeed, I think he loses a very good dinner," interrupted Scrooge's niece. Everybody else said the same, and they must be allowed to have been competent judges, because they had just had dinner; and, with the dessert upon the table, were clustered round the fire, by lamplight.

"Well! I'm very glad to hear it," said Scrooge's nephew, "because I haven't great faith in these young houseKeepers. What do you say, Topper?"

Topper had clearly got his eye upon one of Scrooge's niece's sisters, for he answered that a bachelor was a wretched outcast, who had no right to express an opinion on the subject. Whereat Scrooge's niece's sister—the plump one with the lace tucker: not the one with the roses—blushed.

"Do go on, Fred," said Scrooge's niece, clapping her hands. "He never finishes what he begins to say! He is such a ridiculous fellow!"

Scrooge's nephew revelled in another laugh, and as it was impossible to keep the infection off; though the plump sister tried hard to do it with aromatic vinegar; his example was unanimously followed.

"I was only going to say," said Scrooge's nephew, "that the consequence of his taking a dislike to us, and not making merry with us, is, as I think, that he loses some pleasant moments, which could do him no harm. I am sure he loses pleasanter companions than he can find in his own thoughts, either in his mouldy old office, or his dusty chambers. I mean to give him the same chance every year, whether he likes it or not, for I pity him. He may rail at Christmas till he dies, but he can't help thinking better of it—I defy him—if he finds me going there, in good temper, year after year, and saying Uncle Scrooge, how are you? If it only puts him in the vein to leave his poor clerk fifty pounds, that's something; and I think I shook him yesterday."

It was their turn to laugh now at the notion of his shaking Scrooge. But being thoroughly good-natured, and not much caring what they laughed at, so that they laughed at any rate, he encouraged them in their merriment, and passed the bottle joyously.

After tea, they had some music. For they were a musical family, and knew what they were about, when they sung a Glee or Catch, I can assure you: especially Topper, who could growl away in the bass like a good one, and never swell the large veins in his forehead, or get red in the face over it. Scrooge's niece played well upon the harp; and played among other tunes a simple little air (a mere nothing: you might learn to whistle it in two minutes), which had been familiar to the child who fetched Scrooge from the boarding-school, as he had been reminded by the Ghost of Christmas Past. When this strain of music sounded, all the things that Ghost had shown him, came upon his mind; he softened more and more; and thought that if he could have listened to it often, years ago, he might have cultivated the kindnesses of life for his own happiness with his own hands, without resorting to the sexton's spade that buried Jacob Marley.

But they didn't devote the whole evening to music. After a while they played at forfeits; for it is good to be children sometimes, and never better than at Christmas, when its mighty Founder was a child himself. Stop! There was first a game at blind-man's buff. Of course there was. And I no more believe Topper was really blind than I believe he had eyes in his boots. My opinion is, that it was a done thing between him and Scrooge's nephew; and that the Ghost of Christmas Present knew it. The way he went after that plump sister in the lace tucker, was an outrage on the credulity of human nature. Knocking down the fire-irons, tumbling over the chairs, bumping against the piano, smothering himself among the curtains, wherever she went, there went he! He always knew where the plump sister was. He wouldn't catch anybody else. If you had fallen up against him (as some of them did), on purpose, he would have made a feint of endeavouring to seize you, which would have been an affront to your understanding, and would instantly have sidled off in the direction of the plump sister. She often cried out that it wasn't fair; and it really was not. But when at last, he caught her; when, in spite of all her silken rustlings, and her rapid flutterings past him, he got her into a corner whence there was no escape; then his conduct was the most execrable. For his pretending not to know her; his pretending that it was necessary to touch her head-dress, and further to assure himself of her identity by pressing a certain ring upon her finger, and a certain chain about her neck; was vile, monstrous! No doubt she told him her opinion of it, when, another blind-man being in office, they were so very confidential together, behind the curtains.

Scrooge's niece was not one of the blind-man's buff party, but was made comfortable with a large chair and a footstool, in a snug corner, where the Ghost and Scrooge were close behind her. But she joined in the forfeits, and loved her love to admiration with all the letters of the alphabet. Likewise at the game of How, When, and Where, she was very great, and to the secret joy of Scrooge's nephew, beat her sisters hollow: though they were sharp girls too, as Topper could have told you. There might have been twenty people there, young and old, but they all played, and so did Scrooge; for wholly forgetting in the interest he had in what was going on, that his voice made no sound in their ears, he sometimes came out with his guess quite loud, and very often guessed quite right, too; for the sharpest needle, best Whitechapel, warranted not to cut in the eye, was not sharper than Scrooge; blunt as he took it in his head to be.

The Ghost was greatly pleased to find him in this mood, and looked upon him with such favour, that he begged like a boy to be allowed to stay until the guests departed. But this the Spirit said could not be done.

"Here is a new game," said Scrooge. "One half hour, Spirit, only one!"

It was a Game called Yes and No, where Scrooge's nephew had to think of something, and the rest must find out what; he only answering to their questions yes or no, as the case was. The brisk fire of questioning to which he was exposed, elicited from him that he was thinking of an animal, a live animal, rather a disagreeable animal, a savage animal, an animal that growled and grunted sometimes, and talked sometimes, and lived in London, and walked about the streets, and wasn't made a show of, and wasn't led by anybody, and didn't live in a menagerie, and was never killed in a market, and was not a horse, or an ass, or a cow, or a bull, or a tiger, or a dog, or a pig, or a cat, or a bear. At every fresh question that was put to him, this nephew burst into a fresh roar of laughter; and was so inexpressibly tickled, that he was obliged to get up off the sofa and stamp. At last the plump sister, falling into a similar state, cried out:

"I have found it out! I know what it is, Fred! I know what it is!"

"What is it?" cried Fred.

"It's your Uncle Scro-o-o-o-oge!"

Which it certainly was. Admiration was the universal sentiment, though some objected that the reply to "Is it a bear?" ought to have been "Yes;" inasmuch as an answer in the negative was sufficient to have diverted their thoughts from Mr. Scrooge, supposing they had ever had any tendency that way.

"He has given us plenty of merriment, I am sure," said Fred, "and it would be ungrateful not to drink his health. Here is a glass of mulled wine ready to our hand at the moment; and I say, 'Uncle Scrooge!'"

"Well! Uncle Scrooge!" they cried.

"A Merry Christmas and a Happy New Year to the old man, whatever he is!" said Scrooge's nephew. "He wouldn't take it from me, but may he have it, nevertheless. Uncle Scrooge!"

Uncle Scrooge had imperceptibly become so gay and light of heart, that he would have pledged the unconscious company in return, and thanked them in an inaudible speech, if the Ghost had given him time. But the whole scene passed off in the breath of the last word spoken by his nephew; and he and the Spirit were again upon their travels.

Much they saw, and far they went, and many homes they visited, but always with a happy end. The Spirit stood beside sick beds, and they were cheerful; on foreign lands, and they were close at home; by struggling men, and they were patient in their greater hope; by poverty, and it was rich. In almshouse, hospital, and jail, in misery's every refuge, where vain man in his little brief authority had not made fast the door, and barred the Spirit out, he left his blessing, and taught Scrooge his precepts.

It was a long night, if it were only a night; but Scrooge had his doubts of this, because the Christmas Holidays appeared to be condensed into the space of time they passed together. It was strange, too, that while Scrooge remained unaltered in his outward form, the Ghost grew older, clearly older. Scrooge had observed this change, but never spoke of it, until they left a children's Twelfth Night party, when, looking at the Spirit as they stood together in an open place, he noticed that its hair was grey.

"Are spirits' lives so short?" asked Scrooge.

"My life upon this globe, is very brief," replied the Ghost. "It ends to-night."

"To-night!" cried Scrooge.

"To-night at midnight. Hark! The time is drawing near."

The chimes were ringing the three quarters past eleven at that moment.

"Forgive me if I am not justified in what I ask," said Scrooge, looking intently at the Spirit's robe, "but I see something strange, and not belonging to yourself, protruding from your skirts. Is it a foot or a claw?"

"It might be a claw, for the flesh there is upon it," was the Spirit's sorrowful reply. "Look here."

From the foldings of its robe, it brought two children; wretched, abject, frightful, hideous, miserable. They knelt down at its feet, and clung upon the outside of its garment.

"Oh, Man! look here. Look, look, down here!" exclaimed the Ghost.

They were a boy and girl. Yellow, meagre, ragged, scowling, wolfish; but prostrate, too, in their humility. Where graceful youth should have filled their features out, and touched them with its freshest tints, a stale and shrivelled hand, like that of age, had pinched, and twisted them, and pulled them into shreds. Where angels might have sat enthroned, devils lurked, and glared out menacing. No change, no degradation, no perversion of humanity, in any grade, through all the mysteries of wonderful creation, has monsters half so horrible and dread.

Scrooge started back, appalled. Having them shown to him in this way, he tried to say they were fine children, but the words choked themselves, rather than be parties to a lie of such enormous magnitude.

"Spirit! are they yours?" Scrooge could say no more.

"They are Man's," said the Spirit, looking down upon them. "And they cling to me, appealing from their fathers. This boy is Ignorance. This girl is Want. Beware them both, and all of their degree, but most of all beware this boy, for on his brow I see that written which is Doom, unless the writing be erased. Deny it!" cried the Spirit, stretching out its hand towards the city. "Slander those who tell it ye! Admit it for your factious purposes, and make it worse.

And bide the end!"

"Have they no refuge or resource?" cried Scrooge.

"Are there no prisons?" said the Spirit, turning on him for the last time with his own words. "Are there no workhouses?"

The bell struck twelve.

Scrooge looked about him for the Ghost, and saw it not. As the last stroke ceased to vibrate, he remembered the prediction of old Jacob Marley, and lifting up his eyes, beheld a solemn Phantom, draped and hooded, coming, like a mist along the ground, towards him.

STAVE FOUR

THE LAST OF THE SPIRITS.

Scrooge stood in the darkness, his mind going over the events shown to him by the two Sprits. He felt his mind swimming with images of death, pain and violence. He had seen the attacks of the undead in excruciating detail as well as the fates that awaited those in and around his own home. The horrors in his mind shook him to his core, and with a mighty effort, he forced his eyes open to reveal an ever more terrifying apparition, the dark Spirit.

The Phantom slowly, gravely, silently, approached. When it came near him, Scrooge bent down upon his knee; for in the very air through which this Spirit moved it seemed to scatter gloom and mystery.

It was shrouded in a deep black garment, which concealed its head, its face, its form, and left nothing of it visible save one outstretched hand. But for this it would have been difficult to detach its figure from the night, and separate it from the darkness by which it was surrounded. If he had not already experienced the many forms of terror that the night could bring, he could easily have assumed it was one of the undead itself. There were subtle differences though. The most significant being that this creature stood as a dark and terrible vision with no intention to strike him, just to instil dread and knowledge. In its own way, it was more fearsome than an army of the dead.

He felt that it was tall and stately when it came beside him, and that its mysterious presence filled him with a solemn dread. He knew no more, for the Spirit neither spoke nor moved. It made no attempt to strike or hurt him, but that didn't remove Scrooge's fears.

"I am in the presence of the Ghost of Christmas Yet To Come?" said Scrooge.

The Spirit answered not, but pointed onward with its hand.

"You are about to show me shadows of the things that have not happened, but will happen in the time before us. These will be things that could happen but things I can change if I so wish?" Scrooge pursued. "Is that so, Spirit?"

The upper portion of the garment was contracted for an instant in its folds, as if the Spirit had inclined its head. That was the only answer he received.

Although well used to ghostly company by this time, Scrooge feared the silent shape so much that his legs trembled beneath him, and he found that he could hardly stand when he prepared to follow it. The Spirit paused a moment, as observing his condition, and giving him time to recover.

But Scrooge was all the worse for this. It thrilled him with a vague uncertain horror, to know that behind the dusky shroud, there were ghostly eyes intently fixed upon him, while he, though he stretched his own to the utmost, could see nothing but a spectral hand and one great heap of black.

"Ghost of the Future!" he exclaimed, "I fear you more than any spectre I have seen. But as I know your purpose is to do me good, and as I hope to live to be another man from what I was, I am prepared to bear you company, and do it with a thankful heart. Will you not speak to me?"

It gave him no reply. The hand was pointed straight before them.

"Lead on!" said Scrooge. "Lead on! The night is waning fast, and it is precious time to me, I know. Lead on, Spirit!"

The Phantom moved away as it had come towards him. Scrooge followed in the shadow of its dress, which bore him up, he thought, and carried him along.

They scarcely seemed to enter the city; for the city rather seemed to spring up about them, and encompass them of its own act.

There was something sinister and somewhat terrible about the place though. London was never the greatest jewel in terms of beauty but today it was a changed place. As he swept past the places he knew well he noticed the differences. Some of the houses were gone, entire streets in places razed to the ground as though a great storm had blown them down. Carts moved slowly through the winding alleys, some carried goods but most carried corpses, presumably off to burial. A sullen, bitter mood filtered through the alleys and roads from a miserable and much depleted population.

As they slowed, Scrooge noticed a scream and a group of young men ran in the direction of the noise.

"She's been bitten, quickly, do it!" cried one of them.

A woodsman rushed forward, lifting his light axe he brought it down without hesitation. As the despoiled corpse dropped down the men simply dragged it to one side and heaped it onto one of waiting carts. Scrooge tried to stop to see what was happening, but the Spirit whisked him forwards and past the incident.

A short distance further on and they approached the better, more civilised parts of the city. There were still sections burnt or pulled down but unlike in the slums they were being rebuilt. Small groups of militia rode past, ever on the lookout for the terrible evil that seemed to linger on every street corner. They slowed to a halt as they reached the damaged but still functioning Stock Exchange.

There they were, in the heart of it; on 'Change, amongst the merchants; who hurried up and down, and chinked the money in their pockets, and conversed in groups, and looked at their watches, and trifled thoughtfully with their great gold seals; and so forth, as Scrooge had seen them often.

At first glance, everything looked the way he was accustomed but a second glance revealed some substantial and concerning changes. First, each man was armed. Some carried swords, others pistols and perhaps the more paranoid a mixture of the two. The men were also being watched by a scarred man, possibly an ex sailor or soldier who watched the street with a wary eye. Tucked in his belt were a number of pistols and on his belt a long, curved blade though it was nothing other than a cheap and rusty weapon, probably lost or abandoned many years before. Rust or not the weapon had the potential to cut deeply.

The Spirit stopped beside one little knot of business men. Observing that the hand was pointed to them, Scrooge advanced to listen to their talk.

"No," said a great fat man with a monstrous chin, "I don't know much about it, either way. I only know he's dead."

"When did he die?" inquired another.

"Last night, I believe, some of the creatures managed to break into several of the establishments in his area. Perhaps they were to blame."

"Why, what was the matter with him?" asked a third, taking a vast quantity of snuff out of a very large snuff-box. "He escaped the first outbreak and he hardly stayed to fight like my children did. Shame they did not copy him as they might have lived. When he came back he carried on as normal, I thought he'd never die."

"God knows, maybe one of them broke into his house," said the first, with a yawn.

"Broke into his house, well, they are certainly the only ones that would bother, it is not as though he had possessions of any note or interest. I heard that after the undead were forced out his was the only house not stripped clean by the urchins," said another as he leaned in with a grin.

"You see, his place was already stripped clean, by him!" he laughed.

The rest of the little group erupted into laughter, the only silent man in the group being the rough looking guard, still leaning against the wall and watching the street.

"What has he done with his money?" asked a red-faced gentleman with a pendulous excrescence on the end of his nose, that shook like the gills of a turkey-cock.

"I haven't heard," said the man with the large chin, yawning again. "Left it to his company, perhaps. He hasn't left it to me. That's all I know."

This pleasantry was received with general laughter.

"It is likely to be a very cheap funeral," said the same

speaker; "for upon my life I don't know of anybody to go to it. He had few friends before the attack and they must have all died during it. It is hardly likely he would have bothered to do anything to help them. Suppose we make up a party and volunteer?"

"I have not eaten well in a few days so don't mind going if food is provided," observed the gentleman with the excrescence on his nose. "But I must be fed, if I make one."

Another laugh.

"Well, I am the most disinterested among you, after all," said the first speaker, "for I never wear black gloves, and I never eat lunch. But I'll offer to go, if anybody else will. When I come to think of it, I'm not at all sure that I wasn't his most particular friend; for we used to stop and speak whenever we met. Since the scouring of the city we have had even less contact, though I hasten to add it is hardly a relationship I miss. Bye, bye!"

Speakers and listeners strolled away, and mixed with other groups. Scrooge knew the men, and looked towards the Spirit for an explanation.

The Phantom glided on into a street. Its finger pointed to two persons meeting. Scrooge listened again, thinking that the explanation might lie here.

He knew these men, also, perfectly. They were men of business: very wealthy, and of great importance. Like the small group of merchants and Bankers these two men were well protected. In fact, it seemed excessive, as each man appeared flanked by another. The guardians wore thickened garments on their limbs and carried an array of weapons about their body. Scrooge was at first taken aback by their brash show of weapons in a public street. Then he recalled their descriptions of some great calamity and the number of weapons seemingly carried by men of all classes. It was as though the streets had become a warzone for which every man and woman had to be ready. Scrooge looked away from the weapons and back at the two well-dressed gentlemen. He had made a point always of standing well in their esteem: in a business point of view, that is; strictly in a business point of view.

"How are you?" said one.

"How are you?" returned the other.

"Well!" said the first. "Old Scratch has got his own at last, hey? That makes a dozen in the last month, though in his case none were more deserving."

"So I am told," returned the second. "Cold, isn't it?"

"Seasonable for Christmas time. You're not a skater, I suppose?"

"No. No. Something else to think of. Good morning!"

Not another word. That was their meeting, their conversation, and their parting.

Scrooge was at first inclined to be surprised that the Spirit should attach importance to conversations apparently so trivial; but feeling assured that they must have some hidden purpose, he set himself to consider what it was likely to be. They could scarcely be supposed to have any bearing on the death of Jacob, his old partner, for that was Past, and this Ghost's province was the Future. In his time, Jacob had been a noted man in his field of work much like himself, but the Spirit was hardly likely to have made a mistake and taken him back to visit his old friend was again. Nor could he think of any one immediately connected with himself, to whom he could apply them. It was disheartening to him as he realised how few people he had any connections of note. In fact, the more he thought about it the more he accepted that his work relationships were all that he had. The small numbers of family left had nothing like the darkness that the Spirits had shown he alone possessed.

But nothing doubting that to whomsoever they applied they had some latent moral for his own improvement, he resolved to treasure up every word he heard, and everything he saw; and especially to observe the shadow of himself when it appeared. For he had an expectation that the conduct of his future self would give him the clue he missed, and would render the solution of these riddles easy.

They referred to a man, a coward by any definition, who had abandoned the city during the great crisis and then had returned. It seems there was bitterness by some of the men, as the man had returned when others had not.

It was a thought that Scrooge could well understand. To have left those acquaintances that a man loved or cared for was simply unreasonable. Indeed, how could a civilised gentleman abandon the weak or the poor in such a time as this?

Scrooge snorted to himself, considering that the fate of the man they were watching well deserved. This man was wretched in life and now wretched in death, a fate he seemed to have truly deserved.

He looked about in that very place for his own image; but another man stood in his accustomed corner, and though the clock pointed to his usual time of day for being there, he saw no likeness of himself among the multitudes that poured in through the Porch. He looked for a man of similar stature, perhaps carrying a weapon like the other men he had seen moving about the city. As he looked about, he realised that of course he would not see himself. It gave him little surprise for he had been revolving in his mind a change of life, and thought and hoped he saw his new-born resolutions carried out in this. At this stage, he could be fitter, stronger, dressed in different attire or even off somewhere else. How could he have any idea what he would look like in the Future?

Quiet and dark, beside him stood the Phantom, with its outstretched hand. When he roused himself from his thoughtful quest, he fancied from the turn of the hand, and its situation in reference to himself, that the Unseen

Eyes were looking at him keenly. It made him shudder, and feel very cold.

They left the busy scene, and went into an obscure part of the town, where Scrooge had never penetrated before, although he recognised its situation, and its bad repute. The ways were foul and narrow; the shops and houses wretched; the people half-naked, drunken, slipshod, ugly. Alleys and archways, like so many cesspools, disgorged their offences of smell, and dirt, and life, upon the straggling streets; and the whole quarter reeked with crime, with filth, and misery. As in other parts of the city, there were the carts though in this area there seemed to be far more of them. Bodies dumped upon them though some looked as though they had died from malnutrition rather than violence. Two people rolled in the dirt and as Scrooge looked closer, he noticed one had been bitten, and was going through the later stages of the transformation into the evil walking dead. The other person appeared unhurt and simply going about the business of robbing the soon to be dead person before they turned on him.

Far in this den of infamous resort, there was a low-browed, beetling shop, below a pent-house roof, where iron, old rags, bottles, bones, and greasy offal, were bought. Its doors reinforced with wood and a selection of weapons lay upon every possible entry point. It was a den of iniquity where every soul inside was able and willing to defend it against all intruders. Upon the floor within, were piled up heaps of rusty keys, nails, chains, hinges, files, scales, weights, and refuse iron of all kinds. A stack of loaded pistols and swords untidily placed against the one wall, whilst there were three curved daggers laid out in a curious semi-circle on the floor. Secrets that few would like to scrutinise were bred and hidden in mountains of unseemly rags, masses of corrupted fat, and sepulchres of bones. Sitting in among the wares he dealt in, by a charcoal stove, made of old bricks, was a grey-haired rascal, nearly seventy years of age; who had screened himself from the cold air without, by a frousy curtaining of miscellaneous tatters, hung upon a line; and smoked his pipe in all the luxury of calm retirement. On his side, he carried a foul looking iron rod that had more in common with a cudgel than any military weapon. It was crude and unattractive but functional and well suited to its purpose of keeping the old rascal alive. There was a reason why such a man lived, when younger men suffered to be burnt or buried.

Scrooge and the Phantom came into the presence of this man, just as a woman with a heavy bundle slunk into the shop. But she had scarcely entered, when another woman, similarly laden, came in too; and she was closely followed by a man in faded black, who was no less startled by the sight of them, than they had been upon the recognition of each other. Along with the three strangers came three young boys, each of them armed with a variety of odd weapons. The first carried what looked like a Saracen sword. It was short and curved but when in the boy's hand looked like a weapon in the hands of a Titan. The second boy carried an iron pipe of about a foot long. The third had a staff almost as long as he was tall. The boys stayed close to these adults and moved to protect them as they spotted each other.

After a short period of blank astonishment, in which the old man with the pipe had joined them, they all three burst into a laugh and the three boys moved to the dark edges of the room to watch the appraisal.

"Let the charwoman alone to be the first!" cried she who had entered first. "Let the laundress alone to be the second; and let the undertaker's man alone to be the third. Look here, old Joe, here's a chance! If we haven't all three met here without meaning it!"

"You couldn't have met in a better place," said old Joe, removing his pipe from his mouth. "Come into the parlour. You were made free of it long ago, you know; and the other two an't strangers. Stop till I shut the door of the shop. Ah! How it skreeks! There an't such a rusty bit of metal in the place as its own hinges, I believe; and I'm sure there's no such old bones here, as mine. Ha, ha! We're all suitable to our calling, we're well matched. Come into the parlour. Come into the parlour."

The parlour was the space behind the screen of rags. The old man raked the fire together with an old stair-rod, and having trimmed his smoky lamp (for it was night), with the stem of his pipe, put it in his mouth again.

A screech outside brought an ill chill to the room. As the group fell silent, the three boys rushed to the door, each brandishing his weapon and each wanting to be the first to confront the sound. They waited and the noise faded until silence returned.

"Are we ready?" asked old Joe.

As he spoke they moved closer, the woman who had already spoken threw her bundle on the floor, and sat down in a flaunting manner on a stool; crossing her elbows on her knees, and looking with a bold defiance at the other two.

"What odds then! What odds, Mrs. Dilber?" said the woman. "Every person has a right to take care of themselves. He always did."

"That's true, indeed!" said the laundress. "No man more so."

"Why then, don't stand staring as if you was afraid, woman; who's the wiser? We're not going to pick holes in each other's coats, I suppose?"

"No, indeed!" said Mrs. Dilber and the man together. "We should hope not."

"Very well, then!" cried the woman. "That's enough. Who's the worse for the loss of a few things like these? Not a dead man, I suppose."

"No, indeed," said Mrs. Dilber, laughing.

"If he wanted to keep 'em after he was dead, a wicked

old screw," pursued the woman, "why wasn't he natural in his lifetime? His home was barricaded and locked from the inside and there wasn't the sign of a woman or child anywhere near it. No food of note, it was as a lodger had just arrived and brought nothing but the rags on his back. Such an old, miserable screw. If he hadn't been, he'd have had somebody to look after him when he was struck with Death, instead of lying gasping out his last there, alone by himself. We saw the bite marks, scores of them on his neck, even his arms and legs! It isn't natural."

"It's the truest word that ever was spoke," said Mrs. Dilber. "It's a judgment on him."

"I wish it was a little heavier judgment," replied the woman; "and it should have been, you may depend upon it, if I could have laid my hands on anything else. Of all the places I have visited, this one has to be the worst. It looked like it had been abandoned for weeks, more's the pity else we might have found us something worthy of our time! Now, open that bundle, old Joe, and let me know the value of it. Speak out plain. I'm not afraid to be the first, nor afraid for them to see it. We know pretty well that we were helping ourselves, before we met here, I believe. It's no sin. Open the bundle, Joe."

But the gallantry of her friends would not allow of this; and the man in faded black, mounting the breach first, produced his plunder. It was not extensive. A seal or two, a pencil-case, a pair of sleeve-buttons, and a brooch of no great value, were all. They were severally examined and appraised by old Joe, who chalked the sums he was disposed to give for each, upon the wall, and added them up into a total when he found there was nothing more to come.

"That's your account," said Joe, "and I wouldn't give another sixpence, if I was to be boiled for not doing it. Who's next?"

Mrs. Dilber was next. Sheets and towels, a little wearing apparel, two old-fashioned silver teaspoons, a pair of sugar-tongs, and a few boots. Her account was stated on the wall in the same manner.

"I always give too much to ladies. It's a weakness of mine, and that's the way I ruin myself," said old Joe. "That's your account. If you asked me for another penny, and made it an open question, I'd repent of being so liberal and knock off half-a-crown."

"And now undo my bundle, Joe," said the first woman.

Joe went down on his knees for the greater convenience of opening it, and having unfastened a great many knots, dragged out a large and heavy roll of some dark stuff.

"What do you call this?" said Joe. "Bed-curtains!"

"Ah!" returned the woman, laughing and leaning forward on her crossed arms. "Bed-curtains!"

"You don't mean to say you took 'em down, rings and all, with him lying there?" said Joe.

"Yes I do," replied the woman. "Why not?"

"Weren't you worried the things might come back? What if they had been hiding in the dark places? I told you what happened to Peter, didn't I? He spent too much time working over the old chapel until the priest found him. This man had already been bitten and you know what he did, he paid Peter back for his troubles buy turning him," said Joe incredulously.

"So?" answered the woman.

"You knock me down, you surely do. You were born to make your fortune," said Joe, "and you'll certainly do it."

"I certainly shan't hold my hand, when I can get anything in it by reaching it out, for the sake of such a man as He was, I promise you, Joe," returned the woman coolly. "Don't drop that oil upon the blankets, now. I had to sneak past plenty of unsavoury characters to get these and I don't mind telling you that some of them looked no different to the undead. Maybe they were and maybe they weren't."

"His blankets?" asked Joe.

"Whose else's do you think?" replied the woman. "He isn't likely to take cold without 'em, I dare say."

"I hope he didn't die of anything catching? Eh?" said old Joe, stopping in his work, and looking up.

"Don't you be afraid of that, those creatures had already made short work of him and moved on well before I got there," returned the woman. "I an't so fond of his company that I'd loiter about him for such things, if he did. He is the only man I have seen so despised that he could lie there for weeks without being found. The smell, oh Lord, the smell! Ah! you may look through that shirt till your eyes ache; but you won't find a hole in it, nor a threadbare place. It's the best he had, and a fine one too. They'd have wasted it, if it hadn't been for me."

"What do you call wasting of it?" asked old Joe.

"Putting it on him to be buried in, to be sure," replied the woman with a laugh. "Somebody was fool enough to do it, but I took it off again. No sense wasting it on him, where he's going. If calico an't good enough for such a purpose, it isn't good enough for anything. It's quite as becoming to the body. He can't look uglier than he did in that one. I've seen the walking dead with arms missing and chewing on the flesh of the children that looked prettier than him."

Scrooge listened to this dialogue in horror. As they sat grouped about their spoil, in the scanty light afforded by the old man's lamp, he viewed them with a detestation and disgust, which could hardly have been greater, though they had been obscene demons, marketing the corpse itself.

"Ha, ha!" laughed the same woman, when old Joe, producing a flannel bag with money in it, told out their several gains upon the ground. "This is the end of it, you see! He frightened every one away from him when he was alive, to profit us when he was dead! Ha, ha, ha!"

"Spirit!" said Scrooge, shuddering from head to foot.

"I see, I see. The case of this unhappy man might be my own. My life tends that way, now. Merciful Heaven, what is this!"

He recoiled in terror, for the scene had changed, and now he almost touched a bed: a bare, uncurtained bed: on which, beneath a ragged sheet, there lay a something covered up, which, though it was dumb, announced itself in awful language.

The room was very dark, too dark to be observed with any accuracy, though Scrooge glanced round it in obedience to a secret impulse, anxious to know what kind of room it was. A pale light, rising in the outer air, fell straight upon the bed; and on it, plundered and bereft, unwatched, unwept, uncared for, was the body of this man. On the floor lay a sword, its blade, dark with rust and a thick layer of congealed blood. It looked as though the poor man had fought his last fight and then crept back to bed where he had faced Death alone.

Scrooge glanced towards the Phantom. Its steady hand was pointed to the head. The cover was so carelessly adjusted that the slightest raising of it, the motion of a finger upon Scrooge's part, would have disclosed the face. He thought of it, felt how easy it would be to do, and longed to do it; but had no more power to withdraw the veil than to dismiss the spectre at his side.

He could see the old man's arms lying bloated and pale on the bed, both of which contained bite marks and injuries from some unspeakable evil.

Oh cold, cold, rigid, dreadful Death, set up thine altar here, and dress it with such terrors as thou hast at thy command: for this is thy dominion! But of the loved, revered, and honoured head, thou canst not turn one hair to thy dread purposes, or make one feature odious. It is not that the hand is heavy and will fall down when released; it is not that the heart and pulse are still; but that the hand was open, generous, and true; the heart brave, warm, and tender; and the pulse a man's. Strike, Shadow, strike! And see his good deeds springing from the wound, to sow the world with life immortal!

No voice pronounced these words in Scrooge's ears, and yet he heard them when he looked upon the bed. He thought, if this man could be raised up now, what would be his foremost thoughts? Avarice, hard-dealing, griping cares? They have brought him to a rich end, truly!

A hammer and nails lay near the door and a broken chair nailed across the old timber to block attempts to break in. It was a citadel against the horde and though it may have worked, the inside of the humble house showed nothing but decay.

He lay, in the dark empty house, with not a man, a woman, or a child, to say that he was kind to me in this or that, and for the memory of one kind word I will be kind to him. A cat was tearing at the door, and there was a sound of gnawing rats beneath the hearth-stone. What they wanted in the room of death, and why they were so restless and disturbed, Scrooge did not dare to think. A dark shadow outside could have been a street urchin looking at breaking in to take away the scraps that were left or worse, it could be more of the unholy dead seeking to finish what they had started.

"Spirit!" he said, "this is a fearful place. In leaving it, I shall not leave its lesson, trust me. Let us go!"

Still the Ghost pointed with an unmoved finger to the head.

"I understand you," Scrooge returned, "and I would do it, if I could. But I have not the power, Spirit. I have not the power."

Again it seemed to look upon him.

"If there is any person in the town, who feels emotion caused by this man's death," said Scrooge quite agonised, "show that person to me, Spirit, I beseech you!"

The Phantom spread its dark robe before him for a moment, like a wing; and withdrawing it, revealed a room by daylight, where a mother and her children were.

She was expecting some one, and with anxious eagerness; for she walked up and down the room; started at every sound; looked out from the window; glanced at the clock; tried, but in vain, to work with her needle; and could hardly bear the voices of the children in their play.

At length the long-expected knock was heard. She hurried to the door, and met her husband; a man whose face was careworn and depressed, though he was young. There was a remarkable expression in it now; a kind of serious delight of which he felt ashamed, and which he struggled to repress.

He sat down to the dinner that had been hoarding for him by the fire; and when she asked him faintly what news (which was not until after a long silence), he appeared embarrassed how to answer.

"Is it good?" she said, "or bad?"—to help him.

"Bad," he answered.

"We are quite ruined?"

"No. There is hope yet, Caroline."

"If he relents," she said, amazed, "there is! Nothing is past hope, if such a miracle has happened."

"He is past relenting," said her husband. "He is dead. He was attacked, sometime in the last week or two by some of the walking dead. None of his neighbours noticed but the smell had started to attract attention. When his home was opened they found the bites on his body."

She was a mild and patient creature if her face spoke truth; but she was thankful in her soul to hear it, and she said so, with clasped hands. She prayed forgiveness the next moment, and was sorry; but the first was the emotion of her heart.

"What the half-drunken woman whom I told you of last night, said to me, when I tried to see him and obtain a week's delay; and what I thought was a mere excuse to avoid me; turns out to have been quite true. He was not only very ill, but dying, then and of the undead of all things. You would think a friend or family member would have noticed the symptoms before he entered the fever."

"It is terrible news for his family I am sure, but is it good or bad news for us? To whom will our debt be transferred?"

"I don't know. But before that time we shall be ready with the money; and even though we were not, it would be a bad fortune indeed to find so merciless a creditor in his successor. I doubt we could find a more selfish and vindictive man, even in the whole of London, my dear. We may be poor but we have each other and thanks to this turn of events we may sleep to-night with light hearts, Caroline!"

Yes. Soften it as they would, their hearts were lighter. The children's faces, hushed and clustered round to hear what they so little understood, were brighter; and it was a happier house for this man's death! The only emotion that the Ghost could show him, caused by the event, was one of pleasure.

"Let me see some tenderness connected with a death," said Scrooge; "or that dark chamber, Spirit, which we left just now, will be forever present to me."

The Ghost conducted him through several streets familiar to his feet; and as they went along, Scrooge looked here and there to find himself, but nowhere was he to be seen. As in other parts of the city, there were small groups of yeoman on both mounted and foot patrol. As the alleys and streets became poorer the number of soldiers decreased. Scrooge and the Spirit found themselves forced to the side of one road as a great mass of young men approached. Each one armed with sticks or knives and as they moved on their route, they checked down alleys and entrances to buildings to check for something.

Scrooge stepped back and watched carefully, as he did so quickly worked out that they must be a hastily gathered patrol, probably organised by either the merchants or ruffians to protect their section of the city. As Scrooge relaxed, the Spirit moved forward and swept them both to the steps of an old house. They entered poor Bob Cratchit's house; the dwelling he had visited before; and found the mother and the children seated round the fire.

Quiet. Very quiet. The noisy little Cratchits were as still as statues in one corner, and sat looking up at Peter, who had a book before him. The mother and her daughters were engaged in sewing. But surely they were very quiet!

" 'And He took a child, and set him in the midst of them.' "

Where had Scrooge heard those words? He had not dreamed them. The boy must have read them out, as he and the Spirit crossed the threshold. Why did he not go on?

The mother laid her work upon the table, and put her

hand up to her face.

"The colour hurts my eyes," she said.

The colour? Ah, poor Tiny Tim!

"They're better now again," said Cratchit's wife. "It makes them weak by candle-light; and I wouldn't show weak eyes to your father when he comes home, for the world. It must be near his time."

"Past it rather," Peter answered, shutting up his book. "But I think he has walked a little slower than he used, these few last evenings, mother."

They were very quiet again. At last she said, and in a steady, cheerful voice, that only faltered once:

"I have known him walk with—I have known him walk with Tiny Tim upon his shoulder, very fast indeed."

"And so have I," cried Peter. "Often."

"And so have I," exclaimed another. So had all.

"But he was very light to carry," she resumed, intent upon her work, "and his father loved him so, that it was no trouble: no trouble. And there is your father at the door!"

She hurried out to meet him; and little Bob in his comforter—he had need of it, poor fellow—came in. His tea was ready for him on the hob, and they all tried who should help him to it most. Then the two young Cratchits got upon his knees and laid, each child a little cheek, against his face, as if they said, "Don't mind it, father. Don't be grieved!"

Bob was very cheerful with them, and spoke pleasantly

to all the family. He looked at the work upon the table, and praised the industry and speed of Mrs. Cratchit and the girls. They would be done long before Sunday, he said.

"Sunday! You went to-day, then, Robert?" said his wife.

"Yes, my dear," returned Bob. "I wish you could have gone. It would have done you good to see how green a place it is. But you'll see it often. I promised him that I would walk there on a Sunday. My little, little child!" cried Bob. "My little child!"

He broke down all at once. He couldn't help it. If he could have helped it, he and his child would have been farther apart perhaps than they were.

He left the room, and went up-stairs into the room above, which was lighted cheerfully, and hung with Christmas. There was a chair set close beside the child, and there were signs of someone having been there, lately. Poor Bob sat down in it, and when he had thought a little and composed himself, he kissed the little face. He was reconciled to what had happened, and went down again quite happy.

As with many houses since the crisis, there was a pile of improvised weapons near the doorway. None of the items was suitable for use in warfare but they were certainly suitable for use in the defence of the home against possible incursion by the foul and uncaring walking dead.

They drew about the fire, and talked; the girls and mother working still. Bob told them of the extraordinary kindness of Mr. Scrooge's nephew, whom he had scarcely seen but once, and who, meeting him in the street that day, and seeing that he looked a little—"just a little down you know," said Bob, inquired what had happened to distress him. "On which," said Bob, "for he is the pleasantest-spoken gentleman you ever heard, I told him. 'I am heartily sorry for it, Mr. Cratchit,' he said, 'and heartily sorry for your good wife.' By the bye, how he ever knew that, I don't know."

"Knew what, my dear?"

"Why, that you were a good wife," replied Bob.

"Everybody knows that!" said Peter.

"Very well observed, my boy!" cried Bob. "I hope they do. 'Heartily sorry,' he said, 'for your good wife. If I can be of service to you in any way,' he said, giving me his card, 'that's where I live. Pray come to me.' Now, it wasn't," cried Bob, "for the sake of anything he might be able to do for us, so much as for his kind way, that this was quite delightful. It really seemed as if he had known our Tiny Tim, and felt with us."

"He also mentioned to me that he has been practicing with an old sword and that if we ever needed help with removing a stubborn evil soul or in defence of our home, we simply need to let him know and he'll be here to help us," said Bob.

"I'm sure he's a good soul!" said Mrs. Cratchit.

"You would be surer of it, my dear," returned Bob, "if

you saw and spoke to him. I shouldn't be at all surprised—mark what I say!—if he got Peter a better situation."

"Only hear that, Peter," said Mrs. Cratchit.

"And then," cried one of the girls, "Peter will be keeping company with someone, and setting up for himself."

"Get along with you!" retorted Peter, grinning.

"It's just as likely as not," said Bob, "one of these days; though there's plenty of time for that, my dear. But however and whenever we part from one another, I am sure we shall none of us forget poor Tiny Tim—shall we—or this first parting that there was among us?"

"Never, father!" cried they all.

"And I know," said Bob, "I know, my dears, that when we recollect how patient and how mild he was; although he was a little, little child; we shall not quarrel easily among ourselves, and forget poor Tiny Tim in doing it. He set us an example that we must all ensure we repeat. It is an evil and dangerous world out there and Tiny Tim faced it with bravery, right 'till the end. If only we had been able to save him from the attacks of the street urchins and the undead. We must never fail each other the way many of our neighbours have, if only they had pulled together the way we had, many more people would have lived through that terrible night."

"No, never, father!" they all cried again.

"I am very happy," said little Bob, "I am very happy!"

Mrs. Cratchit kissed him, his daughters kissed him, the

two young Cratchits kissed him, and Peter and himself shook hands. Spirit of Tiny Tim, thy childish essence was from God!

The two left the warmth of the Cratchit home and headed outside and towards an old town hall that was in ruins. At one side, a group or armed urchins were fighting against three walking dead. The fight was brutal and the boys were only able to bring one of the creatures to the ground before they broke and ran in all directions. As the creatures staggered off a small group of militia rode past. They did not stop, simply firing a few shots from their pistols and they continued on their way to something more important and worthy of their time.

Scrooge looked at the violence and then back at the Spirit. He considered the Death all around him, the trouble faced by the Cratchit family and the thing he feared more than the rest, the poor old man that lay dead. The man that lay unwept and unloved.

"Spectre," said Scrooge, "something informs me that our parting moment is at hand. I know it, but I know not how. Tell me what man that was whom we saw lying dead?"

The Ghost of Christmas Yet To Come conveyed him, as before—though at a different time, he thought: indeed, there seemed no order in these latter visions, save that they were in the Future—into the resorts of business men, but showed him not himself. Indeed, the Spirit did not stay for anything, but went straight on, as to the end just now desired, until besought by Scrooge to tarry for a moment.

"This court," said Scrooge, "through which we hurry now, is where my place of occupation is, and has been for a length of time. I see the house. Let me behold what I shall be, in days to come!"

The Spirit stopped; the hand was pointed elsewhere.

"The house is yonder," Scrooge exclaimed. "Why do you point away?"

The inexorable finger underwent no change.

Scrooge hastened to the window of his office, and looked in. It was an office still, but not his. The furniture was not the same, and the figure in the chair was not himself. The Phantom pointed as before.

He joined it once again, and wondering why and whither he had gone, accompanied it until they reached an iron gate. He paused to look round before entering.

A churchyard. Here, then; the wretched man whose name he had now to learn, lay underneath the ground. It was a worthy place. Walled in by houses; overrun by grass and weeds, the growth of vegetation's death, not life; choked up with too much burying; fat with repleted appetite. A worthy place!

The Spirit stood among the graves, and pointed down to One. He advanced towards it trembling. The Phantom was exactly as it had been, but he dreaded that he saw new meaning in its solemn shape.

"Before I draw nearer to that stone to which you

point," said Scrooge, "answer me one question. Are these the shadows of the things that Will be, or are they shadows of things that May be, only?"

Still the Ghost pointed downward to the grave by which it stood.

"Men's courses will foreshadow certain ends, to which, if persevered in, they must lead," said Scrooge. "But if the courses be departed from, the ends will change. Say it is thus with what you show me!"

The Spirit was immovable as ever.

Scrooge crept towards it, trembling as he went; and following the finger, read upon the stone of the neglected grave his own name, Ebenezer Scrooge.

THE LAST OF THE SPIRITS

"Am I that man who lay upon the bed?" he cried, upon his knees.

The finger pointed from the grave to him, and back again.

"No, Spirit! Oh no, no!"

The finger still was there.

"Spirit!" he cried, tight clutching at its robe, "hear me! I am not the man I was. I will not be the man I must have been but for this intercourse. Why show me this, if I am past all hope!"

For the first time the hand appeared to shake.

"Good Spirit," he pursued, as down upon the ground he fell before it: "Your nature intercedes for me, and pities me. Assure me that I yet may change these shadows you have shown me, by an altered life!"

The kind hand trembled.

"I will honour Christmas in my heart, and try to keep it all the year. I will live in the Past, the Present, and the Future. I will take up my sword and move out into the city, and help my brothers in their struggle against this great evil that lurks in the heart of the city. I shall spend my life working for the betterment of all those around me, including myself. None I meet shall suffer the fate that I have seen waiting in store for myself. Whether I can help Tiny Tim, I do not know, but it shall not be from want of trying! The Spirits of all Three shall strive within me. I will not shut out the lessons that they teach. Oh, tell me I may sponge away the writing on this stone!"

In his agony, he caught the spectral hand. It sought to free itself, but he was strong in his entreaty, and detained it. The Spirit, stronger yet, repulsed him.

Holding up his hands in a last prayer to have his fate reversed, he saw an alteration in the Phantom's hood and dress. It shrunk, collapsed, and dwindled down into a bedpost.

STAVE FIVE

THE END OF IT.

The darkness in London was starting to spread by, back at Scrooge's home he came across a miracle.

Yes! and the bedpost was his own. The bed was his own, the room was his own. Best and happiest of all, the Time before him was his own, to make amends in!

"I will live in the Past, the Present, and the Future!" Scrooge repeated, as he scrambled out of bed. "The Spirits of all Three shall strive within me. Oh Jacob Marley! Heaven, and the Christmas Time be praised for this! I say it on my knees, old Jacob; on my knees!"

He was so fluttered and so glowing with his good intentions, that his broken voice would scarcely answer to his call. He had been sobbing violently in his conflict with the Spirit, and his face was wet with tears.

"They are not torn down," cried Scrooge, folding one of his bed-curtains in his arms, "they are not torn down, rings and all. They are here—I am here—the shadows of the things that would have been, may be dispelled. They will be. I know they will!"

He looked out through the window to see the rise of the calamity. In the distance, a series of thick black plumes marks the fires or violence near the ports.

His hands were busy with his garments all this time; turning them inside out, putting them on upside down, tearing them, mislaying them, making them parties to every kind of extravagance.

"I don't know what to do!" cried Scrooge, laughing and crying in the same breath; and making a perfect Laocoön of himself with his stockings. "I am as light as a feather, I am as happy as an angel, I am as merry as a schoolboy. I am as giddy as a drunken man. A merry Christmas to everybody! A happy New Year to all the world. Hallo here! Whoop! Hallo!"

He had frisked into the sitting-room, and was now standing there: perfectly winded.

"There's the saucepan that the gruel was in!" cried Scrooge, starting off again, and going round the fireplace. "There's the door, by which the Ghost of Jacob Marley entered! There's the corner where the Ghost of Christmas Present, sat! There's the window where I saw the wandering Spirits! It's all right, it's all true, it all happened. Ha ha ha!"

Really, for a man who had been out of practice for so many years, it was a splendid laugh, a most illustrious laugh. The father of a long, long line of brilliant laughs!

"I don't know what day of the month it is!" said Scrooge. "I don't know how long I've been among the Spirits. I don't know anything. I'm quite a baby. Never mind. I don't care. I'd rather be a baby. Hallo! Whoop! Hallo here!"

He was checked in his transports by the churches ringing out the lustiest peals he had ever heard. Clash, clang, hammer; ding, dong, bell. Bell, dong, ding; hammer, clang, clash! Oh, glorious, glorious!

Running to the window, he opened it, and put out his head. No fog, no mist; clear, bright, jovial, stirring, cold; cold, piping for the blood to dance to; Golden sunlight; Heavenly sky; sweet fresh air; merry bells. Oh, glorious! Glorious!

"What's to-day!" cried Scrooge, calling downward to a boy in Sunday clothes and, who seemed to be in a hurry, which was odd based on his clothing.

"Eh?" returned the boy, with all his might of wonder.

"What's to-day, my fine fellow?" said Scrooge.

"To-day!" replied the boy. "Why, Christmas Day, sir, but it doesn't matter so. They say the demons have returned and the army is trying to keep them out of the city, sir."

"It's Christmas Day!" said Scrooge to himself. "I haven't missed it. The Spirits have done it all in one night.

They can do anything they like. Of course they can. Of course they can. Hallo, my fine fellow!"

Scrooge seemed impervious to the comments from the boy as he delighted in life and the fact that he had the chance to make amend, to make his life in the image of something new and good.

"Hallo!" returned the boy, though he looked confused at the man's apparent unwillingness to understand the terrible events unfolding.

"Do you know the Poulterer's, in the next street but one, at the corner?" Scrooge inquired.

"I should hope I did," replied the lad.

"An intelligent boy!" said Scrooge. "A remarkable boy! Do you know whether they've sold the prize Turkey that was hanging up there?—Not the little prize Turkey: the big one?"

"What, the one as big as me?" returned the boy.

"What a delightful boy!" said Scrooge. "It's a pleasure to talk to him. Yes, my buck!"

"It's hanging there now," replied the boy.

"Is it?" said Scrooge. "Go and buy it."

"Walk-er!" exclaimed the boy.

"No, no," said Scrooge, "I am in earnest. Go and buy it, and tell 'em to bring it here, that I may give them the direction where to take it. Come back with the man, and I'll give you a shilling. Come back with him in less than five minutes and I'll give you half-a-crown!"

The boy looked around him as though he expected some evil to take him and then without further hesitation he was off like a shot. He must have had a steady hand at a trigger who could have got a shot off half so fast.

"I'll take it to Bob Cratchit's!" whispered Scrooge, rubbing his hands, and splitting with a laugh, before stopping and thinking.

"Good Lord, I remember now. Poor Cratchit and his family are at this very moment trapped and fighting for their lives in their home," he said, as he recalled his previous experience of Mr Cratchit barricading the door of his home against the horde.

"Well, his family is certainly going to need a hearty meal if they are to survive this day, and I have every intention of making sure they do!"

He moved to the wall that carried the odd assortment of relics and weapons. The first looked just like the old sword that Mr. Jenkins had shown him so many years before. He pulled it down and withdrew the blade. It was dark and pitted but sturdy and still sharp, even after this long time of abandon. Next to the sword was a small dagger that he ducked into his trousers and a duelling sword of a type known as a smallsword that looked like a thin, pointed fire poker. As he examined the weapons, a series of shouts and screams came from the street. He rushed outwards, grabbing his thick coat on the way.

"What is happening?" he shouted, as some stricken

people darted past him and along the road. A young boy looked towards him as his mother grabbed and yanked him away. Scrooge looked to the right and spotted the danger, the undead were here and they had already made their way from the docks and into the heart of the city.

"What did the Ghost say?" he muttered to himself, trying to recall what he had seen in his experiences with the Spirits.

"Why yes, the creatures are being controlled by some malevolent beast looking to bring ruin to the city. The Spirit said there was something in the Bank that they were drawn to, an object from across the seas that was responsible for their evil intent and power."

Scrooge stopped and looked whimsical as though an idea of great import and peculiarity had entered his mind.

"Yes, of course. I will stop these creatures and with that will ensure Christmas stays the way it always should be. First things first though, I must endeavour to make certain Cratchit and his family are safe, then I will resolve the situation at the Bank," he said wryly before adding, "and it is perhaps time to rectify certain inequities."

Staggering up the road the first party of the dead approached him. They were just like the creatures he had encountered seven years prior, but unlike at that time these monsters appeared to have a purpose. Off into the distance he could see other groups taking different routes though the city, almost like a team of cleaners working through a large house.

"Good Lord, they plan to empty or kill every soul in the city!" exclaimed Scrooge.

He looked down to the scabbard of the light cavalry sword and withdrew the dull blade. It was heavy in his hand and without any effort seemed to drop down at the tip as though it had a will of its own to cut. Scrooge looked up and centred his attention on the three zombies now only twenty feet from him.

"Come on you devils!" he shouted as he shuffled towards them, holding the sword up high to his right shoulder.

As he reached the first creature, he noticed it wearing a docker's clothing and even carried some tools on it. Some poor worker must have fallen victim to these most evil of creatures. Looking at its face, the eyes were pitted and sunken and its mouth dripped a congealed and foul looking blood. The skin was pale and lifeless and the creature moved as though another person was twisting and contorting its limbs.

With a single bold movement, Scrooge brought the blade down in a cutting motion that instantly transformed him back to decades earlier. The blade slashed into the creature's shoulder, keeping the movement until it left its body just below the ribs. As the blade dropped down Scrooge stepped forward and lifted it back to deliver another downwards cut but this time from the left. The two cuts formed an X shape on the creature and before he had returned the sword to his right shoulder, the creature started its collapse.

The other two zombies moved forward, each reaching out to grab at Scrooge. He stepped back, almost stumbling as he gave ground. With several quick cuts, he slashed into the arms of his attackers but other than causing cursory damage, they continued their progress towards him.

"Stop damn you!" shouted Scrooge as his cuts became more erratic.

The closest zombie now grabbed Scrooge's arm and its grip was stronger and more powerful than he could possibly have imagined. Pain shot up through his muscles and the reflex action caused him to open his hand. The sword dropped down to the floor and, in a brief moment, the two creatures were on him. He fought back as hard as his frail body would allow but he simply was not strong enough to hold off the two of them. One moved closer, exposing its foul fangs and the blood infused drool that ran from its mouth. Scrooge looked down in fear but spotted the small dagger he had pushed into his belt earlier. He pushed his elbow up into the closest creature's throat to give him some advantage and then grabbed the dagger. Without thought, or hesitation, he stabbed it into the thing's throat in an upward motion that must have forced the point into the base of the back of the brain.

It was as though somebody had blown on the wick of

a candle. The creature's eyes flickered and life vanished from the body. It collapsed to the ground as though an invisible hand had been holding it up to walk and move. Spurred on by his success Scrooge pushed the remaining monster from him and then stepped back himself giving him a little space to move. He spotted his sword lying on the ground and grabbed for it. The zombie was almost upon him but was not speedy enough. With one swift horizontal cut, he slashed the thing's head clean from its shoulders. The head toppled off and the body slumped lifelessly to the ground.

Behind the body stood two children, both young boys and both in absolute awe. The first boy carried the bird that Scrooge had asked him to buy earlier.

"Mr. Scrooge, sir!" said the first.

"Where did you learn that?" asked the second.

Scrooge straightened his back and tried to retrieve his breath before speaking to the boy.

"A long, long time ago from an old soldier. Where are you both going?" he asked, out of interest, and surprise, being as everybody else was abandoning the streets.

"We heard that a group of foreigners are bring something into the city, any person that becomes near it is attacked by those dark, unholy things," said the first boy.

"My brother was bitten by one in the dark just two hours ago, sir. He had a fever and died. Then he awoke from death and attacked my sister. That's when the rest of us scarpered, sir," said the second.

Scrooge considered the situation for a moment. It occurred to him that he could never stop them placing the object at the sacred site in the heart of the city all by himself. He needed help from people that cared enough to put themselves in danger for others.

More people ran past, some dropping their goods as they ran but none slowed down, they simply continued as fast as they could, shouting, crying and screaming.

"Boys, we need to stop this. Do you want to be forced out of your own town by this group of thieves and filth?" he asked sternly

"No, sir. How can we do anything, sir?" asked the first boy.

"Boy, you know the home of Mr Cratchit?" he asked.

"Yes, sir, the gentleman who works here?" answered the boy.

"Find your friends and tell them to meet there in ten minutes, not a minute more. We shall create an army of good people and we will march on the Bank. We will fight our way inside and destroy that which the evil wishes to reach."

The two boys looked at each other in confusion, not understanding the point old Scrooge was making.

"Listen, I have seen this object before, it is evil and will destroy all we know and love. I am not able to explain how, but I know it will bring ruin to this place for years to come. Bring your family, your friends and all you can find. Arm yourselves with pans, knives or anything else you can acquire. You will be like Lord Uxbridge and his heavy cavalry, riding to the rescue. Now go, young boys, with haste!" he cried.

The two boys excitedly rushed away towards their homes, leaving Scrooge with a sword in one hand and the great bird in another.

Picking up his feet, Scrooge ambled down the street and towards Cratchit's home. It was a bizarre sight, as the old man appeared to be impervious to the gloom of the city as those inhabitants continued to stream by. One man, of similar age stopped, recognising Scrooge.

"Good day, sir," he said in surprise.

Scrooge slowed and glanced up and down at the man. A moment of realisation dawned on him as he recognised the man from his visions of the future. It was one of the gentlemen who said he had said hello to Scrooge on many a day.

"A good day it is indeed, Sir!" said Scrooge as he hurriedly shook the man's hand.

Scrooge made to move away but the man held on to him with a puzzled expression on his face.

"But, sir, have you not seen the evils entering the city? We must leave forthwith," he said.

"Humbug, sir, humbug!" said Scrooge with a glint in his eye. "I say we gather up the good citizens and we resolve to defeat the confounded horde this very day. Already the young boys and urchins are assembling just a few roads away. We will leave in not more than five minutes to the heart of this problem!" he said with great gusto.

"But, sir, what do you know of this evil?" asked the befuddled man.

"I have seen its face and I have fought it before. Trust me my good man, if you join me you will help to make this Christmas Day one that is always remembered."

The man looked about, noticing a small number of people watching their conversation. A few more continued to run past, but an even greater number stood by.

"I saw him fighting them just now, he killed a group of them and he's just an old man!" shouted one.

"Old man indeed!" laughed Scrooge. "Think what we could do together. We will drive them out, as the rain drives the filth from the streets. Are you with me, good people?" he cried.

A great cheer rose up in the street from over thirty people that had gathered.

"Grab any weapon you can and follow me!" he cried, and shouting they moved off towards Cratchit's home. Each of the crowd grabbed any item they could to use as a weapon. Some grabbed rocks, others pieces of timber and some a mixture of labouring tools. As they moved on they encountered more terrified people. These poor souls slowed and then stopped in amazement to see the small, scruffy army of people marching behind Scrooge. As they rounded the final corner, Scrooge could see the Cratchit home and it was not a minute too soon. In front of the house was a group of at least twenty of the walking dead. Off behind these in the distant gloom an even larger group staggered ever closer.

"Here they are good people of London. Will you see them take your homes, your friends and your families?" shouted Scrooge.

"No!" came the reply in unison from the swelling ranks.

"Follow me!" shouted Scrooge and with a swing of his sword, he rushed ahead as fast as he could.

With a crash, he hit the first of the zombies and then proceeded to hack and slash with great vigour. As each cut came down onto the head of a creature, Scrooge felt his zeal and strength returning. It was as though life was breathing back into his shell. For a moment he could have been overwhelmed, but for the small group of vagabonds and youths that jumped out from the dark alleys nearby and joined in the fight. They were small but far from weak and with each strike that Scrooge delivered, another ten came from the young boys.

"Come!" shouted the gentleman that Scrooge had so recently seen scorning him in the future.

"Will you let common children such as these deny you of your chance to cleanse this place?" he added.

With a deft move, he withdrew a slender and sophisticated looking sword. It had much in common with a traditional court sword, and though lacking in any discernable edge its tip was sharp and it was well constructed. From inside his coat pocket he withdrew a small pistol and with a cry rushed headlong into the fight.

Before long the entire street looked like some ancient battlefield, as one by one the local inhabitants opened their doors and joined the fray, men with their axes and woman carrying pots and pans. In less than a full minute the horde of creatures lay battered and crushed, and all for the loss of not one person. As the people paused catching their breath, the door to old Bob Cratchit's home opened and he stepped out, holding a metal poker in one hand. He looked terrified and had evidently been struggling against these fiends for some time. He looked at the armed group and held out his weapon in front of him, expecting an attack at any moment.

"I will not let you in!" he shouted.

"Mr Cratchit, old boy! It is me, your friend Scrooge!" came a shout from the centre of the mass of people.

"Scrooge?" he asked in surprise.

He pushed forward of the crowd, now dripping in sweat and still carrying the wrapped bird under his arm. He moved up to the man and handed him the concealed item.

"Something for you and your dear family!" he said a

grin. "I am sorry it took so long."

Mr Cratchit opened up the brown paper and peered inside, spotting the massive, tasty looking bird before looking back at Scrooge.

"I, I don't know what to say," he said in surprise.

"Say nothing, my good man. I could do with your help though," he said as he waved over to the crowd of people

Mrs Cratchit moved to the open door and looked out, surprised to see Scrooge stood there.

"Mr Scrooge has brought us a fine gift," said old Bob Cratchit, as he handed the mighty bird over to his wife.

She peeked inside, still stunned by the crowd and the arrival of such a gift.

"We must be off, this group of creatures is just one of many, they are making their way to the Bank, just like they did when old Jacob met his end, God rest his soul," said Scrooge as he stepped back.

"You are going to fight them?" said an incredulous Mr Cratchit.

"Yes, and if you would join us I would be honoured," Scrooge replied.

Turning to his wife and children, he spoke briefly and then after hugging his children he pushed the door shut behind him. Jumping down into the street, he moved up to the front of the crowd where Scrooge stood waiting.

"I'm here, sir, what did you have in mind?" he asked.

Scrooge turned to the people and raised his sword in

the air.

"To the Bank!" he cried.

He turned to Mr Cratchit, "I'll explain my little plan on the way," he said.

As they rounded the corner, they encountered two more zombies who were beating incessantly on some poor soul's door. Scrooge did not even have to act; the number of the men at the front leapt into action and smashed them both to the floor. They all moved on and swelled in numbers as those in their homes felt it would be safer to stay with them, rather than trapped in their homes waiting for Death.

"These creatures are controlled by some foul artefact from overseas. There is a sacred spot below the Bank, in fact where years ago a mysterious and sinister cult used to worship. If the artefact is placed there it will allow its owner to take control of this horde, and command them at will. Until that happens only those creatures very near to the object can be fully controlled," he explained.

"Jacob and I saw it years ago and the Keepers very nearly managed to use it. Thankfully, the militia arrived in time and drove it away. This time I fear they may already be close, look!" said Scrooge, as he pointed down one of the alleys. At the far end, he could see the parallel street to the one they followed. A group at least as large as theirs staggered along, presumably heading to the Bank.

"Why don't we just find the Keepers and stop them

before they reach the Bank?" asked Mr Cratchit.

"A fine question, my boy, and one that is simply answered, where are the Keepers? Yes, they brought it here but how do we find them? The only thing we know for certainty is that the Bank is where they must take it. If we can take control of the Bank and stop them from placing the item in its place at the heart of the old temple, we can stop them and perhaps destroy the artefact once and for all," explained Scrooge.

The group continued their march, now more a small army and their numbers still swelled to more than two hundred souls. As they moved on Scrooge looked back proud of the spirit of his companions, and of what they had achieved with just a little effort and courage. Three children came running from a side alley and up to Scrooge.

"Mr, they are just over the hill, you should turn back!" said one.

"Yes, you'll all be killed!" said another.

"Not with Mr Scrooge with us!" shouted one of the boys in the small army.

They moved past the three children who upon seeing such a mighty host quickly fell in at the rear and followed. If nothing else, they preferred the company of large numbers to the hiding out in the shadows, waiting for help that likely would never arrive.

They reached the summit and the front line slowed and then stopped. From their position, they could see the open square in front of the Bank was an open battle. A mixture of the undead, local people and the odd soldier were fighting a bloody battle and it was clear the increasing number of undead were winning. From the front of the Bank a small group of militia were trying to fight their way out of the broken door, but only a handful remained and the weight of numbers were soon to push them inside. Several fires burned in the street, a column of smoke rose up from a broken structure nearby.

"They must have already placed the object in its evil place!" shouted Scrooge.

He turned to his group of volunteers.

"I have seen this object before now, it is fragile and can be destroyed. We need to break through their line and fight our way inside. We must be strong and make our way into the catacombs to where the object lies. Once it is smashed, its power will be lost and these creatures will lose their master's control. They will not suddenly die but they will lose their plan and will be much easier to beat. Are you ready to end this?" he shouted as he lifted his curved sword high into the air.

"Let 'em have it!" shouted one of the boys who rushed off, closely followed by several of his friends.

"Charge!" shouted Scrooge.

With a roar, the crowd surged down the hill and towards the swirling melee. The boys struck the creatures first and with both speed and agility managed to slip past whilst delivering sniping strikes with their weapons. Mr Cratchit and Scrooge, plus a group of older men, pushed on to the right and started to work their way through a thick throng of the zombies. As Scrooge slashed downwards, the others pushed and stamped. One of the men was dragged down, and it looked as though his fate was sealed. Just in time though, a woman knelt down and struck the creature with a pan, the force of the impact knocking the creature backwards. As it landed on its back, another man jumped in and thrust a sharpened piece of wood into its torso.

Inside the Bank was the small number of surviving soldiers that the creatures had pushed inside the building, and were stuck in a tiny group, each trying desperately to protect the flank of the next. One by one they were dragged to the ground until only the three strongest remained.

Bob Cratchit reached the broken door and pushed inside. Two men followed him and then Scrooge chased behind them. With a cut and slash, they broke through the first group of dead and reached the three soldiers.

"Who are you?" shouted the largest soldier, as he swung his curved blade and brought down another creature.

Scrooge leapt forward and hacked down two as he reached the man.

"Scrooge, and we are here to destroy the artefact."

"How do you know about it?" asked the second soldier, whilst pushing back two zombies.

"Does it matter?" asked Mr Cratchit. "We need to get there, and fast, or the city will be overrun!"

Scrooge leaned forward and shouted to the tallest soldier.

"We will take care of this, you need to get reinforcements to clear up their survivors when we succeed," said Scrooge.

"Succeed? You are only a few people!" said the third soldier.

Part of the doorframe collapsed, and through the dust emerged at least twenty more people who rushed in to hack and stab at the undead that were still moving up from the secret underground vault in the Bank.

"Look, there are more outside, this is our chance," shouted Scrooge.

He turned from the soldier, and towards the dark opening, he knew to lead underground. As he moved forwards, he called to the others around him.

"Come, to the crypt!"

The open area of the Bank only contained a dozen or so zombies, and they were quickly dispatched, by Scrooge's people as they headed to the steps. The soldiers rushed the door, and in the small window the fight had created, were able to slip outside and into the darkness of the alleys. As they left the building a small number of the undead trickled inside, each one seeming to know exactly where the one, true threat remained.

As the three soldiers sneaked away, the tallest turned

back and watched in amazement, as the creatures appeared to close ranks around the Bank. There must have been two or three hundred of them and they formed a thick band of growling death. The local people had fallen back and resorted to hurling objects at the horde though none seemed to want to tangle with such a large and now uniform mass of creatures.

"I hope they know what they're doing," said the taller soldier.

"It doesn't matter, we can't help them yet. We need to get the lads here and quickly," said the second.

The soldiers nodded almost in unison and then turned and rushed away though as they moved they were careful to avoid the odd creature making its way to the square.

Inside the Bank, the small group of Scrooge's followers moved down the stairs and into the underground chamber. It was slightly different to the way he had seen it in his visitations by the Spirits. Icons and imagery hung from the walls and columns, and candles burned in almost every corner of the place. For a moment, it gave the impression of a wondrous grotto full of sparkling lights and wonders. In the centre stood group of twelve men in red, just like the ones Scrooge had seen in his glimpses of the Past. They stood around the item, presumably the artefact.

"Behind us!" cried one of the boys, as he was struck and tumbled down the stairs.

As the noise from their arrival awoke the interest of the

Keepers of the artefact, they drew their weapons. Before moving, several of them threw knives or used short bows and then they charged. The first impact of these missiles brought three poor souls to the ground, one certainly dead and the other two were seriously hurt.

Though Scrooge's group outnumbered the Keepers, they were nowhere near the level of skill of these men. A furious melee broke out with only Scrooge being able to offer the enemy more than token resistance. In less than a minute of fighting, they had lost another five. They were down to just two dozen people able to carry on. Three of the men in red tried to separate Scrooge from the group, but he would not be so. As the first approached, he hacked for his head. The man, well used to fighting with a blade moved it to intercept, but was tricked. It was a simple feint from an old man! As his opponent lifted his weapon in defence, Scrooge slashed the man from the thigh to the chest. The rest of his people rallied around him and they tried to push back the group of men in red.

As the battle continued on, another three of the Keepers died. There were eight of them and those that remained were the strongest and fastest. Scrooge had reached to within ten feet of the artefact when he was seen. It was as though something clicked in their heads as they realised the precious item was in danger. Abandoning the battle, they all swept in to stop Scrooge. From the staircase, at least a dozen of the undead had made it inside and were working their way down to the swirling fight. Two boys, both armed with newly collected swords from the dead Keepers did their best to slow them down.

Scrooge on the other hand seemed possessed. As he swung his blade he was deftly assisted by Mr Cratchit and a group of children and adults determined to fight these evil men. The fight was long and brutal and before long only ten of Scrooge's party remained, whilst the Keepers' number whittled down to five.

The gentleman, to whom Scrooge had seen in his vision of the future, was still there and remarkably good with his sword and walking stick. As he stabbed one of the Keepers in the shoulder, he noticed a gap and leapt forward towards the artefact. Scrooge, seeing the man moving ahead tried to help but the fast moving blades stopped him. As the man reached down, he grasped the artefact and placed his hands upon it.

"Destroy it, destroy it now!" cried Scrooge and he desperately hacked another of the Keepers to the ground.

The old man looked confused and stumbled backwards as though afraid of Scrooge or perhaps the Keepers. As he retired, his hands slipped off the artefact. Two of the evil men stepped back and faced him, both with their wicked blades held aloft. Yet none would attack him. As this extraordinary event unfolded, the rest of the fight slowed and then stopped, the two groups staring, waiting for the old man to do something.

The zombies, who had now entered the chamber were just a short distance away and had stopped. They stood silently, as though waiting for an order.

"What is happening?" asked Mr Cratchit.

"It is the artefact. Whoever touches it controls the dead. Good Lord, sir, you must have the power now!" cried Scrooge.

The old man, still clutching his stick and sword dropped to his knees in fear.

"My eyes!" he screamed, "I can see them!"

As he turned and moved, the undead seemed almost to mimic him. It was clear that the dark powers of the artefact had turned him into the Master of the Dead, though what he would do was anybody's guess.

The boy, the one that just a short while ago had bought the great bird, slid neatly between the legs of the Keepers and, without hesitating brought his weapon, a simple broom handle down hard onto the artefact, still placed in its box. As the weapon struck a crack flash erupted from the case and a shockwave like a blast of wind tore through the room. The Keepers cried out and rushed for the staircase, abandoning the shattered relic and both the undead that still lurked. The zombies started to move though they lacked the control or coordination they seemed to have before.

"Good work, my boy, you've broken the link, look!" cried Scrooge.

The tired group watched incredulously as the zombies staggered about, each one uncertain as to what to do.

"Finish them, my boys, clear the room!" shouted Scrooge.

With one last push, they rushed about the place, each cutting and hacking until every last one of the creatures was still.

Scrooge, the old man and Mr Cratchit moved over to the shattered relic and looked down at its pieces. The old man moved to pick them up but Scrooge stopped him.

"Be careful, we do not know if any power remains," said Scrooge, as he moved to a burning lantern on the wall and brought it towards the remains of the relic.

"You, lend me your handkerchief," ordered Scrooge.

A man in his early twenties handed over a small piece of cloth with which Scrooge carefully scooped up the pieces and deposited them in the broken wooden box.

"Collect anything you can find that burns and bring it here!" called Mr Cratchit.

In just a few minutes, the group had erected a small bonfire over the relic. Without hesitation, Scrooge lowered the torch and started the fire. In took a few minutes for the fuel to take hold and then it burned furiously as though its heart were naphtha itself. As the flamed burnt though the box the fingers of red flame changed to blue, then green and then a screech, like the sound of a harp echoed in the room. The flame returned to normal and in a few minutes the relic, the box and all the fuel reduced to ash.

Scrooge placed his sword in its scabbards and turned to the survivors.

"A great piece of work my friends, you have done great deeds," he explained with a look of joy.

A mighty roar like the sound of a war horn bellowed from outside and reached the underground chamber and with it a great cry of triumph. Scrooge was at the stairs first and close behind him were the rest, some of them helping to carry the wounded to the surface. They reached the floor of the Bank and found it deserted. Without waiting, they surged outside, expecting to find the horse and a raging battle. Instead, they ran out to see a group of several dozen mounted soldiers who were in the square and waving their swords in the air. On the ground were scores of bodies from the undead horde.

Even better, the wounded seemed to be getting better and those that appeared near death saw life returning to them.

"The darkness must have left them, the spread has stopped," said Bob Cratchit.

"Indeed it has!" said Scrooge with a smile.

"How about the young lady in my home? Will she be safe or will she turn?" asked a worried Bob Cratchit.

"Look around you, it is over. The fight has been won and it is time to celebrate!" said a joyful Scrooge.

Scrooge was better than his word. He did it all, and

infinitely more; and to Tiny Tim, who did not die, he was a second father. The young boy spared the ravages of the disaster that could have befallen London. He became as good a friend, as good a master, and as good a man, as the good old city knew, or any other good old city, town, or borough, in the good old world. Some people laughed to see the alteration in him, but he let them laugh, and little heeded them; for he was wise enough to know that nothing ever happened on this globe, for good, at which some people did not have their fill of laughter in the outset; and knowing that such as these would be blind anyway, he thought it quite as well that they should wrinkle up their eyes in grins, as have the malady in less attractive forms. His own heart laughed: and that was quite enough for him.

As for the artefact, Scrooge never again heard anything of the item or the shards rumoured to have been scattered. No signs of the undead were heard of again, and before long their very existence became nothing more than mystery or myth.

He had no further intercourse with Spirits, but lived upon the Total Abstinence Principle, ever afterwards; and it was always said of him, that he knew how to keep Christmas well, if any man alive possessed the knowledge. May that be truly said of us, and all of us! And so, as Tiny Tim observed, God bless Us, Every One!